Otogizōshi:
The Fairy Tale Book
of
Dazai Osamu

Otogizōshi:
The Fairy Tale Book
of
Dazai Osamu

Translated by
Ralph F. McCarthy

Introduction by
Joel Cohn

Kurodahan Press
2011

Otogizōshi: The Fairy Tale Book of Dazai Osamu
Translated by Ralph F. McCarthy

Translation copyright © 2011 Ralph F. McCarthy
Introduction copyright © 2011 Kurodahan Press

FG-JP0030-L2.1
ISBN-13: 978-4-902075-40-3
ISBN-10: 4-902075-40-7

WWW.KURODAHAN.COM

Acknowledgements

I would like to thank Dazai Osamu for being, like, my favorite writer ever; Kita Morio for turning me on to Dazai many years ago; Edward Lipsett for suggesting we do this book and then shepherding it all the way through to completion; Joel Cohn for his terrific introduction and for pointing out a number of embarrassing gaffes and mistranslations; Sakai Akinobu for patiently elucidating passages that had me baffled; Nancy H. Ross for her excellent editing; Mary McCarthy and Fred Walton for their perspicacious critiques of the manuscript; Poe Ballantine (greatest living American novelist) for his advice and encouragement; and YOU, dear reader, for giving this book a chance. I hope you like it. I and I alone am responsible for any and all mistakes and infelicities.

R.F.M.

Table of Contents

Introduction

Joel Cohn

The air raids that devastated most of the large and me-
dium-sized cities of Japan in the final year of World War
II form a decidedly unconventional backdrop for Dazai
Osamu's retellings of four well-known Japanese folk tales.
As Dazai's prologue indicates, he composed these stories
in the spring and early summer of 1945 as the increasingly
frequent air raids, which had begun in November of 1944,
were adding an element of more or less constant danger
to the already difficult lives of the residents of Tokyo and
other Japanese cities, many of whom had nothing more to
rely on in the way of protection than hastily dug backyard
trenches. After evacuating his wife and two young children to his wife's hometown of Kōfu in late March, Dazai
returned alone to his house on the western outskirts of
Tokyo, only to see it damaged by bombs in early April.
He then rejoined his family in Kōfu, where he completed
The Fairy Tale Book shortly before losing his home to an
air raid for a second time. Despite the chaotic conditions
that prevailed in the months preceding and following Japan's surrender in mid-August, the book was published in

October, making it one of the first works of literature to appear after the end of the war.

In the less than three years that remained before the drowned bodies of Dazai and a mistress were discovered, apparently in the aftermath of a double suicide, he burst forth from relative obscurity to become the first great literary sensation of postwar Japan. His best-known works from these years, especially the novels *The Setting Sun* (1947) and *No Longer Human* (1948), not only vividly captured the pervasive sense of misery and emptiness that gripped a ruined nation, they also secured him an enduring place in the Japanese literary pantheon and a seemingly unshakable reputation as Japan's preeminent voice of gloom and suffering, rendered in an unflinchingly honest and unforgettably vivid style.

To many, including some who have never actually read anything by him, Dazai is a virtual poster boy for the stereotype of the modern Japanese novelist as a tormented spirit, a suicide waiting to happen, and the mere mention of the titles of his best-known works is enough to evoke images of all-encompassing despair. But even at its grimmest, his writing is regularly illuminated with flashes of sardonic wit, and in much of it, especially the pieces from the middle years of his relatively brief career, the sense of angst is muted and his penchant for subtle comedy is deftly displayed. *The Fairy Tale Book* can be seen as a culmination of this brighter (or at least less miserable) strain in Dazai's fiction. Even as it immediately confronts us with a tension-laden tableau of a family huddling in an air raid shelter, the prologue offers a surprisingly droll depiction of the slightly feckless-sounding narrator's attempts to deflect his wife's complaints and placate a child too young to understand the peril they face. The stories themselves offer only occasional hints of having been composed at a time when the lives of the Japanese people were becoming increasingly desperate—not that a more candid portrayal of the looming threat of disaster would have been approved by the censors.

Turning to traditional Japanese materials was an attractive option for writers during the war years, as they afforded a source of relatively safe subject matter and met the government-imposed mandate for writing that conformed to "national policy" as long as they were handled with proper respect. Dazai had already produced a number of pieces in this vein, but he was rarely one for playing along with authority figures of any kind. In *The Fairy Tale Book* the apparent mood of reverence for national tradition is periodically undercut as the storyteller notes the difficulty of confirming the accuracy of his sources while cowering in a bomb shelter, points out the failure of some of his characters to embody the time-honored spirit of the samurai, or undermines his purported stance of "deference for the sanctity of the Japanese historical record" with long-winded displays of playful pseudo-pedantry. Most revealingly of all, he explains that he was forced to abandon his plan to provide some momentary diversion for "those fighting courageously to help Nippon through her national crisis" by retelling the stirring tale of the demon-conquering hero Momotarō (a favorite figure during the war years) once he realized that "a completely invincible hero just isn't good story material" and that "An author who has never been number one in Japan—or even number two or three—can hardly be expected to produce an adequate picture of Japan's foremost young man."

As some of these comments suggest, Dazai was also a writer with a compulsive urge to reflect, or even project, his real-life experiences and concerns in his work. In other words, he was very much a representative of the predilection for autobiographical or self-referential semifiction, known as *shishōsetsu*, which exerted a powerful hold on many Japanese authors and readers for much of the twentieth century. In these stories he often seems to be encouraging us to draw no dividing line between the author and the teller, occasionally even going so far as to refer to himself by his own name. But here the more directly autobiographical elements, which form the main or even the sole story line in so many other works by Dazai, are confined to the storyteller's intermittent evocations of wartime conditions and his own personal situation in his introductory and concluding comments, along with his periodic interruptions and digressions, creating a kind of parallel narrative to the tales that he is recounting.

For Japanese readers this addition of a new angle to long-familiar stories is likely to provide a large part of the fun. But for many of them, the pleasure of reading Dazai is as much about getting a feeling of being in touch with the author as it is about being drawn into the world of a story, and in these tales Dazai's distinctive voice is very much in evidence, reaching out and taking us into his confidence in a warm, intimate tone. Far more often than a conventional storyteller might, he persistently provides his own running commentary on the main events of the tales—sometimes trying to extract a meaning, sometimes wandering off on a tangent that relates more to his own preoccupations than it does to any events in the story. We may not know, or care, whether the "real Dazai" indeed lived through moments like those he describes here, or whether he actually believed everything the storyteller claims to believe, but as in the tales that were told to us as children, the voice and presence of the teller, by turns reassuring, fearsome, and clownish, and occasionally wise, is as much a part of the experience as the incidents and characters themselves.

This is not the only way in which Dazai transforms the traditional tales. He fleshes out the bare bones characterizations and situations of the children's storybook versions (shown in the translation in bold type), giving each of the sketchily described stock figures of the originals a context and a distinctive personality. Most of these have little or no relation to the traditional story line, and some, such as the garrulous, wisecracking tortoise of "Urashima-san" and the disastrously gendered tanuki and rabbit of "Click-Clack Mountain," are truly memorable. Many of them are endowed with a degree of psychological complexity and ambiguity that owes more to the techniques of modern fiction than to the simplistic good or evil characterizations of conventional folk tales; this is particularly apparent in the final story, "The Sparrow Who Lost Her Tongue," where the strengths and flaws of the husband and wife are depicted with deep sensitivity and understanding.

Dazai's retellings also introduce a number of themes that play little or no part in the originals. Some of these will be familiar to readers who know other works of his: the quandary of the outsider who is taken seriously by nobody and misunderstood by everybody, including himself; the family and male-female ties, including marriage, that become emotional dead ends rather than sources of comfort or fulfillment; and the suspicion that things are all too likely to go wrong when people are left to their devices, or as the narrator puts it in the conclusion to "The Stolen Wen," "although not a single instance of wrongdoing occurs in the story, people end up unhappy." "The Sparrow Who Lost Her Tongue" offers one of the most succinct distillations of Dazai's outlook to be found anywhere in his work: "The people of this world are all liars. . . . All they do is lie. And the worst part of it is that they don't even realize they're doing it."

While readers familiar with the conventional versions of the tales may appreciate the note of freshness and increased depth created by Dazai's innovations, those who come to them with a preformed idea of what to anticipate (or dread) from this author are likely to find that the fantasy world settings and characters provide a degree of relief and distancing from real-world predicaments. But unlike what we see in some better-known Dazai works, the outcomes here are not inevitably tragic; the narrator's conclusion, as he struggles to derive some kind of meaning from the seemingly nonsensical goings-on of "Wen," that the tale is a "tragicomedy of character," might well be applied to the collection as a whole. One also notes the presence of some benign themes that are rarely expressed so explicitly in his other writing. One of these is the emphasis on acceptance and desirelessness seen in three of the four stories, most prominently in the princess's ideal of "divine resignation" in "Urashima-san" and the "gift of oblivion" through which she confers her own state of grace on the hero, which the narrator cites as an example of "the profound compassion that permeates Japanese fairy tales." The stoic acceptance of loneliness in "The Stolen Wen" and the moments of silent recognition and tacit acknowledgement of gratitude at the end of "The Sparrow Who Lost Her Tongue" also resonate powerfully with the plight of an author and readers struggling to make their way through an ongoing calamity, with an uncertain outcome that they can do nothing to affect.

Another striking theme is the recurring appearance of refuges and utopias—the mountain forest in "The Stolen Wen," where the old man goes to seek relief from his grim home life and finds a crew of happy-go-lucky ogres carousing; the undersea palace in "Urashima-san," where you are free to do whatever you want without criticism; and the birds' lodge in the bamboo grove in "The Sparrow Who Lost Her Tongue," where another frustrated husband finds the warm companionship that is missing at home. None of these fantasy spaces provides a permanent escape, but in each case the protagonist is able to return home transformed, having found a kind of peace and better able to accept the vicissitudes that real life continues to throw at us. This cautiously reassuring note is all the more powerful for being sounded amidst those days and months of peril and fear. Dazai's ability to rise to the occasion in this way is a main reason why these uniquely fractured, reassembled, and amplified fairy tales offer us something richly delectable and rare not only in his own writing but in all of modern Japanese literature—or even literature as a whole. We are lucky to have them. Enjoy!

Otogizōshi:

The Fairy Tale Book

of

Dazai Osamu

Prologue

"Ah! There they go."

The father lays down his pen and climbs to his feet. A warning siren won't budge him, but when the antiaircraft guns start roaring, he secures the padded air-raid hood over his five-year-old daughter's shoulders, takes her in his arms, and carries her to the bomb shelter in the garden. The mother is already huddled inside this narrow trench, their two-year-old son strapped to her back.

"Sounds pretty close, eh?" the father says to her.

"Yes. It's awfully cramped in here."

"You think?" he says in an aggrieved tone. "But this is just the right size, really. Any deeper and you run the risk of being buried alive."

"It could be a little wider, though, couldn't it?"

"Mm. Maybe so, but the ground's frozen right now. It's not that easy to dig. I'll get to it," he promises vaguely, in hopes of ending the discussion so he can hear news of the air raid from a neighbor's radio.

No sooner have the mother's complaints subsided, however, than the five-year-old begins demanding they leave the trench. The only way to quiet this one is to open a picture book. *Momotarō, Click-Clack Mountain, The Sparrow Who Lost Her Tongue, The Stolen Wen, Urashima-san* . . . The father reads these old tales to the children.

Though he's shabbily dressed and looks to be a complete fool, this father is a singular man in his own right. He has an unusual knack for making up stories.

Once upon a time, long, long ago . . .

Even as he reads the text in a strangely imbecilic voice, another, somewhat more elaborate tale is brewing inside him.

The Stolen Wen

**Once upon a time, long, long ago,
there lived an old man
with a great big wen on his cheek.**

This old man, this Ojī-san, or "Grandfather," lived at
the foot of Mount Tsurugi in Awa Province, on the island
of Shikoku. At least, I believe that's correct, but I have
no reliable source material at hand to back me up. I seem
to recall that this story of the stolen wen originated in *A
Collection of Tales from Uji*, but it's impossible to consult
the old texts in a homemade bomb shelter. I face a similar problem with the tale following this one, "Urashima-
san," the facts behind which were first reported in the
ancient *Chronicles of Japan*. A long poem about Urashima
and his journey to the Dragon Palace is included in the
Manyōshū; and there are what appear to be versions of
his tale in the *Chronicles of Tango Province* and *Lives of
Japanese Immortals*, not to mention, in more recent times,
Ōgai's well known play. And didn't Shōyō or someone
devise a dance routine based on the story? In any case, we
all know that our beloved Urashima-san lives on in any
number of entertainments, from noh and kabuki plays to

5

geisha hand dances. I've never had anything resembling a library of my own, however, because I sell or give away books as soon as I've read them. When wanting to get my facts straight, therefore, I have to hit the streets, following my own uncertain memory in an attempt to track down a text I recall once having read, but I can't even do that now, you see. I'm crouching in a hole in the ground, and the only piece of literature available to me is this picture book balanced on my knees. Consequently I am compelled to forego the careful perusal of original texts and to content myself with whatever might unwind in my own imagination. But perhaps that will only make for a more lively and entertaining story. . . .

So goes the sour-grapes-like justification with which this odd person, the father, reassures himself as he resumes:

Once upon a time, long, long ago . . .

And as he reads the words aloud, wedged inside the shelter, he inwardly paints a new and altogether different tale.

This Ojī-san of ours loves saké. Most drinkers are lonely men, isolated in their own homes. To ask whether they drink because they're isolated or isolated because the rest of the family disapprove of their drinking would be like clapping and trying to decide which hand made the sound—it can only lead to a lot of vain quibbling. In any case, although there's nothing particularly problematic about his family situation, a cloud always hangs over Ojī-san at home. His wife, whom we'll call Obā-san, or

"Grandmother," is very much alive and well. She's closing in on seventy, but her back is straight, her eyes clear. It's said that she was once quite a beauty. A quiet and serious sort from girlhood on, she now goes about her housework each day with grim determination.

"Well, spring has sprung!" Ojī-san burbles. "The cherry trees are in bloom."

"Is that so," Obā-san responds without interest. "Will you get out of the way, please? I'm trying to clean up here."

Ojī-san slumps in his seat, deflated.

He also has a son, who is nearly forty and so morally irreproachable as to be a rarity in this world. This son not only neither drinks nor smokes but makes a point of never laughing or getting angry or experiencing pleasure either. All he does each day is silently toil in the fields, and since the people in the village and surrounding areas have little choice but to respect him for that, he's known far and wide as the Saint of Awa. He has never married or shaved his beard, and one is tempted to wonder if he isn't made of wood, or stone.

In short, this family of Ojī-san's is nothing if not respectable and upstanding. And yet the fact remains that he is depressed. He wants to be considerate of his family but feels he cannot help but drink. And if drinking at home only leaves him all the more dispirited, it's not because either Obā-san or the Saint of Awa has ever scolded him for it. They sit at the table with him each evening, eating their dinner in silence as he sips his saké.

Growing a bit tipsy, Ojī-san begins to desire conversation and to make inane comments. "By the way, spring is here at last, you know. The swallows are back." An uncalled-for observation. "'Spring evening: one moment, a thousand pieces of gold,' what?" he mutters. Utterly insipid.

"*Gochisōsama de gozarimashita.*" The Saint of Awa, having finished his dinner, stands up and bows deeply as he intones these words of gratitude for the meal.

"Ah," Ojī-san says, and sadly drains his little saké cup. "Guess I'll eat something myself."

So it generally goes when he drinks at home.

**One fine morning, Oji-san went up
the mountain to gather wood.**

On sunny days, he likes to wander the forested slopes of Mount Tsurugi with a gourd dangling from his waistband, collecting kindling at his leisure. When he grows a bit tired of picking up sticks, he sits with loosely crossed legs on a large boulder and clears his throat with a great display of self-importance.

"*Ahem!* What a view!" he says, and sips saké from his gourd. He looks happy. Away from home like this, he seems a different person. He might even be unrecognizable if not for the enormous wen on his cheek. Some twenty years ago, in the autumn of the year he passed the half-century mark, his right cheek had begun to feel warm and itchy, and then to swell little by little. As he patted and stroked it, the wen grew ever larger, and he would smile sadly and say, "Now I've got myself a fine grandchild."

To which his son, the Saint of Awa, would reply with great joy-killing solemnity, "A man's cheek cannot give birth to a child."

Obā-san, for her part, proclaimed without so much as a reassuring smile that the wen didn't appear to be life-threatening, and showed no further concern. The neighbors were somewhat more sympathetic, saying that such a large wen must be quite a nuisance and how had he acquired it and wasn't it painful? But Ojī-san just laughed and shook his head. Far from considering the wen a nuisance, he really has come to think of it as a darling grandchild, a companion to comfort him in his solitude, and when he washes his face each morning he takes special care to purify the wen with cool, fresh water. On days like today, when his spirits are high and he's drinking alone in the mountains, this wen is an indispensable sidekick. He's petting it fondly as he sits atop the boulder with his legs crossed wide.

"Ha! What's there to be afraid of? I'll have my say! You're the ones who need to drink and loosen up a little. There's such a thing as being too serious, you know. 'The Saint of Awa,' eh? Well, forgive *me*, mister holy man!"

He mutters these tirades to his wen, roundly disparaging one person or another, and always finish by clearing his throat loudly: *Ahem!*

It grew cloudy.
The wind started to blow.
Rain came pouring down.

Squalls like this are rare in springtime. But we must assume that weather is volatile on mountains the size of

Tsurugi. White mists rise from the mountain slope as rain beats down, and pheasants and other birds dart for cover with the swiftness of arrows. Ojī-san just smiles to himself.

"Can't hurt to cool off my wen in a little shower," he says, and remains sitting on the rock, watching the rain come down. But the longer he watches, the harder it rains, and the less it looks like letting up.

"Hmm. Now it's gone beyond cool," he concedes. Standing up, he sneezes mightily, then shoulders the bundle of wood he's gathered and crawls into the brush. It's already crowded in there with birds and beasts taking shelter.

"Excuse me! Coming through! Sorry!" He greets the monkeys and rabbits and pheasants and things with cheerful courtesy and passes deeper into the forest, where he finally wriggles inside the hollow trunk of an enormous old cherry tree.

"Well, well, this is a very nice room!" he says once inside, then calls to the rabbits and the others, "Come on in, everyone! There aren't any high and mighty Obā-sans or Saints in here! Come in, come in!" He babbles excitedly for a while, but soon he's softly snoring. Drinkers tend to say inane and obnoxious things when they're drunk, but most of them are in fact harmless, innocent souls like this.

Waiting for the rain to stop,
    Ojī-san fell fast asleep.
The skies cleared, and the sun went down.
Now a bright moon lit up the cloudless sky.

It's a waning quarter moon, the first one of spring. It floats in a sky the color of water, almost a pale green, and slivers of moonbeam litter the forest floor like pine needles. Ojī-san is still sound asleep. Only when a cloud of bats flies out of the hollow tree with a thunderous flapping of wings does he wake with a start, alarmed to find that it's nighttime.

"Uh-oh. This isn't good." The somber face of his old woman and the austere countenance of the Saint rise before his eyes. "Never yelled at me yet," he reminds himself. "But coming home this late, things could get unpleasant. Say! Saké's not gone, is it?" He shakes the gourd and takes heart when he hears a faint *plish-plash*. "There you are!" He drains the last drops and begins to feel tipsily sentimental. "Well, I see the moon's out," he says, and continues to mumble fatuous remarks to himself as he crawls out from the hollow tree. "Spring evening: one moment—"

And then . . .

**Whose voices were those,
    laughing and shouting?
Oh, look! What a wondrous sight!
    Was it a dream?**

In a grassy clearing in the forest, an otherworldly scene is unfolding. Just look . . .

Now, I don't really know what these ogres, these *Oni*, are like, never having met any. From childhood on, I've seen more pictures of Oni than I care to remember, but I have yet to be granted the privilege of coming face to face with one. Complicating matters is the fact that there would appear to be many varieties of Oni. We use the

11

word to describe hateful people, murderers, and even vampires, and one might therefore feel safe in assuming that these beings possess, in general, fairly despicable personality traits. But then one spies in the "New Books" column of the newspaper a headline reading, "The Latest Masterpiece from the Ogre-like Genius of So-and-So-*sensei*," and one is perplexed. One wonders if the article is an attempt to alert the public to So-and-So-sensei's wicked influence or evil machinations. Worse yet, they have gone so far as to label him the "Oni of the Literary World." One would think that the great sensei himself would react angrily to being called such nasty and insulting names, but apparently that isn't the case. One even hears rumors to the effect that he secretly encourages their use, which only leaves one—at least one as ignorant as I—even more perplexed. I simply can't bring myself to conceive of these Oni creatures—with their tiger-skin loincloths, scarlet faces, and crude iron clubs—as gods of art.

But perhaps this is only my lack of experience talking; perhaps Oni come in a wider variety than I'm aware of. If only I had an *Encyclopedia Nipponica* at hand, I could easily assume the guise of a respectable scholar, admired by women of all ages (as most academicians tend to be), and with a look of unfathomable profundity on my face hold forth at great length and in minute detail on the subject of Oni, but, unfortunately, I'm crouching in a bomb shelter, and the only volume I have at my disposal is this children's book on my lap. I am obliged to base my argument entirely on the illustrations.

Just look. In a fairly wide, grassy clearing deep in the forest, twelve or fifteen gigantic, red-faced, heteromorphous beings sit in a circle, dressed in those unmistakable tiger-skin loincloths, drinking together beneath the light of the moon.

Ojī-san is momentarily paralyzed with fear. But drinkers, though cowardly and quite useless when not drinking, are apt to display when drunk a courage that few non-drinkers can summon. Right now, Ojī-san is feeling his rice wine. We have already witnessed the fearless and heroic manner in which he rails against his stern missus and his morally irreproachable son when they aren't around. Nor does he disgrace himself now, after crawling out from the tree on all fours and being stopped in his tracks by the eldritch spectacle before him. He observes the dubious drinking party carefully for some moments. And then something like joy bubbles up in his heart.

"Looks like they're really enjoying that wine," he murmurs.

It seems that drinkers derive a certain pleasure even from watching others get drunk. Perhaps, then, most lovers of drink are not what we today would call egoists but rather guardians of the sort of generous spirit that inspires all of us to toast, at times, our neighbor's happiness. We do this because we want to drink, yes, but if our neighbor gets drunk along with us, our pleasure is double. Ojī-san knows what he's seeing. He knows intuitively that those hulking red figures before him, neither human nor beast, are in fact of the fearsome tribe known as Oni. The tiger-skin loincloths alone are enough to dispel any doubts he might have. But these ogres are getting happily sloshed. Ojī-san too is sloshed, and he can't help but feel a certain sense of fellowship. Still on all fours, he watches the uncanny proceedings unfold in the light of the moon.

As far as he can see, Oni—or at least *these* Oni—show no signs of possessing the tortured, twisted minds of homicidal maniacs or bloodthirsty vampires. Their faces are red and frighteningly grotesque, to be sure, but they seem to him cheerful, easygoing fellows for all that. And, fortunately, this judgment of his turns out to be more or less on the mark. These are of an exceedingly gentle breed we might almost describe as the hermit Oni monks of Mount Tsurugi, and they have little in common with your average demons from hell. They aren't carrying those dangerous iron clubs, for starters; that alone should be evidence enough that they have no malice in their hearts. But unlike the Seven Hermit Sages who fled to the Bamboo Grove with knowledge far beyond that of ordinary mortals, these hermit Oni are simpletons.

Someone once explained to me a lame-brained theory to the effect that since the Chinese character "wizard" consists of the elements "person" and "mountain," anyone who lives in a remote mountainous area deserves to be called a wizard. If we stretch a point and accept this hypothesis, then perhaps these hermit Oni of Mount Tsurugi, however deficient they might be in intellect, are worthy of being called wizards as well. In any case, such a term seems a good deal more appropriate than "ogres" for this particular group of scarlet giants drinking mindlessly in the moonlight.

I have described them as simpletons, and now they are justifying that description by celebrating in ways that display an appalling lack of artistic talent or sensibility— screeching and howling meaninglessly, slapping their knees and roaring with laughter, or rising to their feet and leaping and spinning around and around. One of them even curls into a ball and rolls about, bouncing back and forth from one edge of the circle to the other. Surely such exhibitions constitute proof that phrases like "Ogre-like Genius" and "Oni of the Literary World" make no sense whatsoever. One simply cannot credit the notion that these talentless goofballs are somehow divinely inspired.

Ojī-san too can only shake his head at the pathetic level of Oni dancing skills.

"That is some very bad dancing indeed! Mind if I teach you a few moves?"

Ojī-san loved to dance.
He couldn't help himself.
He ran into the circle and started dancing.
His wen bounced up and down.
It was fun to watch, and funny too!

Ojī-san is full of liquid courage. And because he also feels a certain bond with these Oni, he's not the least bit afraid as he springs into the center of the circle and begins performing the traditional Awa festival dance and singing in a fine, clear voice:

Young ones wear Shimada hairdos,
old ones wear their wigs!
Who can see those red, red ribbons
and not lose his mind?
Married ladies, don your hats,
come along and dance, dance!

The Oni are absolutely delighted. They make a ca-cophony of strange noises—*Kya, kya*! *Keta, keta*!—and laugh till tears roll down their cheeks and drool drips

from their chins. Encouraged by their reaction, Ojī-san
tries another verse.

Once we got beyond the valley
  all we saw was rocks!
Once we got past Sasa Mountain,
  only bamboo grass, oh!

Really belting out the final lines, he finishes his comical, light-footed dance with a flourish.

The Oni were overjoyed.
"He must dance for us again,
  at the next moonlight bash!"
"Let's keep something valuable of his,
  to make sure he comes back!"

So says one of them, and they all put their heads together for a grunt-filled discussion. They seem to come,
in their stupidity, to the conclusion that Ojī-san's bright,
shiny wen is a rare treasure, and they decide that if they
keep it, he's sure to return. They're ignorant, yes, but after
living deep in the mountain forest for so long, perhaps
they have indeed learned some of the wizardly arts: they
pluck the wen clean from Ojī-san's cheek, leaving not so
much as a scar, or any other trace.

Ojī-san is stunned.

"Wait! You can't take that! It's my grandchild!" he
cries, but the only response is a triumphant cheer.

Morning came.
Dew glistened on the mountain path.
Ojī-san walked homeward,
  rubbing his smooth, flat cheek.

Ojī-san's wen has been his only confidant, and he's conscious of a certain loneliness without it. But the early morning breeze doesn't feel so bad tickling his suddenly unencumbered cheek. *Guess I came out more or less even. Something lost, something gained. What's on the plus side here? Well, I danced and sang my heart out for the first time in ages. . . .* Such are his generally optimistic thoughts as he makes his way home. Along the path he bumps into his son, the Saint, who's just heading out to the fields.

"*Ohayō gozarimasu.*" The Saint removes the kerchief that covers his mouth to solemnly intone his somewhat countrified morning greeting.

"Well, well," is all Ojī-san manages to say. He's thoroughly flustered, and the two of them part ways with no further exchanges. Seeing that his father's wen has disappeared overnight, the Saint is inwardly somewhat puzzled, but since he believes that to offer any manner of critique of one's own parent's features is to stray from the true path, he pretends not to notice.

When Ojī-san reaches home, his wife calmly and rotely welcomes him back, without even touching upon the question of where he's been all night. "The miso soup is cold," she mutters under her breath as she sets the table for his breakfast.

"That's all right. I'll eat it cold. No need to warm it up." Ojī-san shrinks guiltily into himself as he sits down. He's dying to tell his wife about all the marvelous things that happened last night, but in the stern and austere atmosphere of her presence he finds the words sticking in his throat. He eats with head bowed, feeling perfectly wretched.

"It looks like your wen has dried up," she says, in her matter-of-fact way.

"Mm." Ojī-san has lost the will to speak.

"It must have broken open," she says indifferently. "Water came out, I suppose?"

"Mm."

"It'll probably fill up again," she says.

"I guess."

In the end, Ojī-san's wen is not a matter of much concern to his family. There lives in the same neighborhood, however, another old man with a similarly large and bothersome wen. This old man's wen is on his left cheek, and he considers it an unspeakable nuisance and firmly believes that it has held him back in life. He looks in the mirror several times each day and bitterly thinks of all the laughter and scorn he has had to endure since youth, just because of this wen. He once grew a beard in an attempt at camouflage, but, sadly, the red dome of the protuberance peeked out from his new white whiskers like the sun rising amidst the foamy waves of the sea, creating an even more spectacular prospect.

Let us note, however, that aside from the wen there is nothing repellent or questionable about this old man's appearance or bearing. He is powerfully built, with a prominent nose and piercing eyes. He speaks and comports himself in a grave and dignified manner and always gives the impression of being sensible and discriminating. He dresses meticulously and is said to be well educated and to possess a fortune far beyond anything the drunken Ojī-san, for example, could ever dream of; and everyone in the neighborhood holds him in the highest regard, referring to him as "Sir" or even "Sensei."

In short, the old gentleman is blessed in many ways, but that large, jiggly wen on his left cheek makes it impossible for him to enjoy his good fortune. Because of the wen, in fact, he suffers from a chronic melancholia. His wife is surprisingly young—just thirty-six. She is not especially pretty but fair-skinned and plump, and she's always laughing in a cheerful if somewhat crass way. They have a daughter of twelve or thirteen, a lovely but rather impertinent child. The mother and daughter are very close and forever giggling together, so that in spite of the husband's perpetual scowl, the household impresses one as being full of sweetness and light.

"Mother, why is Father's wen so red?" The impertinent daughter expresses herself frankly and freely, as always. "It looks like the head of an octopus."

"Ho, ho, ho, ho!" Far from scolding her daughter, the mother just laughs. "It does! That, or a polished coconut shell."

"Shut up!" the old gentleman shouts. He leaps to his feet, glaring at his wife and child, then retreats to a dimly lit chamber in the rear of the house, where he peers into the mirror.

"Damn this thing," he mutters.

He's begun to consider slicing the wen off with a knife—so what if it kills him?—when he catches wind of the news that the old drunk from down the street has been mysteriously relieved of the same affliction. That evening he slips out to visit the drunken Ojī-san's thatched hut, where he hears the whole story of that mysterious moon-light drinking-party.

"This is wonderful news!" he said.
"I'll have them take *my* wen too!"

The old gentleman is thoroughly braced. Fortunately, there's a moon tonight as well. He sets out with a glint in his eye and his lips tightly pursed in an inverted V, like a samurai scurrying to the front. *Tonight I shall demonstrate for those foul ogres a dance that will leave them gasping in stunned admiration. And if by any chance they aren't stunned, I shall lay them all low with this iron-ribbed fan! What are they, after all, but drunken, dimwitted Oni?*

Such are his ardor and enthusiasm as he makes his way deep into the mountain forest with shoulders squared, clutching his fan in his right hand, that it's difficult to tell whether he wants to dance for the ogres or exterminate them. When an artist is pumped up with the intention of creating a masterpiece, however, the work generally comes out poorly, and this is to be the case with the old gentleman's performance. He's so frightfully inflated that it's destined to be an utter disaster. He steps solemnly and reverently into the circle of wine-guzzling Oni and clears his throat.

"Inexperienced though I may be at this sort of thing . . ." Saying only this much to introduce his art, he flips open his iron-ribbed fan with a flourish and strikes a pose, glaring unflinchingly up at the moon. After several long moments of this, he lightly taps the ground with one foot and slowly begins to moan his song:

I am a monk, passing the summer
at Naruto in Awa . . . .

With that, he turns ever so slowly, then once again freezes in position, glaring up at the moon.

The Oni were puzzled and frightened.
One by one they jumped up and fled
back into the forest.

"Wait a moment!" the old gentleman shrieks, and chases after them. "You can't leave me now!"

"Run! Run! It's Shōki, Queller of Demons!"

"No, no! That's not who I am!" The old gentleman finally catches up to and prostrates himself before one of the Oni, clinging to its leg. "Please, I beg of you! My wen!"

"What? The wen?" The Oni, confused by all the excitement, misunderstands him. "That's a treasure we were holding for the other old man, but—all right, you can have it. But no more dancing like that, please! You ruined a perfectly good drunk, and now we've got to find a new spot and start all over. Let go of me! Hey, somebody give this crazy old man that wen from the other night! He says he wants it!"

The Oni attached the other wen
to his right cheek.
Now the old man had two wens,
one dangling from each side of his face.
How heavy they looked as he
trudged back to the village!

What a sad ending. You have to feel sorry for the second old man. Most of our children's stories end with the perpetrators of evil deeds getting what's coming to them, but this old gentleman did nothing wrong. He tried to perform a dance that, owing to a case of nerves, turned out rather disturbingly weird, but that's the extent of his crime. Nor was anyone in his family particularly evil. And the same can be said for the saké-loving Ojī-san and his family, and for the Oni of Mount Tsurugi as well. None of them did anything wrong. And yet, although not a single instance of wrongdoing occurs in the story, people end up unhappy.

It's difficult, therefore, to extract from this tale of the stolen wen a moral lesson for daily life. But were an indignant reader to demand to know why, in that case, I even bothered to write the damn thing, I would have no choice but to reply as follows: It's a tragicomedy of character. At issue here is an undercurrent that winds through the very heart of human existence.

Urashima-san

Apparently a man named Urashima Tarō actually lived once, long ago, in a place called Mizunoe, on the Tango Peninsula in what is now northern Kyoto Prefecture. They tell me you can still find a shrine dedicated to Tarō there, in a poor little village on the coast. I've never visited the place myself, although I understand it's about as desolate a stretch of beach as you're likely to find.

At any rate, that's where our Urashima Tarō resides. He doesn't live alone, of course, but with his mother and father. Also a younger brother and sister. Not to mention a large number of servants. He is, you see, the eldest son of an old and highly respected family. Now, eldest sons of respected families have had, from ancient times to our own, a certain characteristic in common: namely, a sense of style. Some might describe this stylishness favorably, as refinement, and others less favorably, as prodigality. But in Tarō's case the prodigality, if it can be so called, was of a sort entirely distinct from that associated with wine and women and what have you. Among second and third sons one often finds that variety of prodigal who overindulges in liquor and pursues women of lowly birth, muddying his own family's name in the process, but the number one son is generally quite innocent of such abominable behavior. Because he is responsible for the wealth and property accumulated by his ancestors, the first-born male comes naturally to acquire a certain steadfast stodginess and to conduct himself in an impeccably proper and genteel manner. Rather than the intense floozies-and-booze version favored by his younger brothers, therefore, the eldest son's prodigality is more of a sideline, a series of frivolous diversions. All he asks of these diversions, furthermore, is that they cement his reputation for possessing the taste and gentility that befit his station in life.

"Dear brother, you just don't have any sense of adventure," the younger sister, an impertinent thing of sixteen, tells him one day. "That's what's wrong with you."

"No, that's not it," their coarse and rebellious eighteen-year-old brother chimes in. "He's too pretty, is what it is."

The younger brother is dark-complected and strikingly ugly.

But Urashima Tarō never loses his temper, even when tested with such uninhibited criticism from his younger siblings. "To allow one's curiosity to get the better of one is a sort of adventure," he tells them. "And to control one's curiosity is also a species of adventure. Both are risky propositions. There is a thing called destiny to which all men are subject."

Exactly what he means by these words is anyone's guess, but after pronouncing them with a calm, composed, and enlightened air, he clasps his hands behind his back and strolls out to the seashore. There, ambling aimlessly along the beach, he mutters fragments of refined and elegant poetry.

24

Scattered by the wind
like the tattered ends
of a worn rush mat—
the fishing boats!

"Why can't people get along without criticizing one another?" Urashima shakes his head as he ponders this rudimentary question. "Never have the bush clover blooming on the beach, nor the little crabs who skitter o'er the sand, nor the wild geese resting their wings in yonder cove found fault with me. Would that human beings too were thus! Each individual has his own way of living. Can we not learn to respect one another's chosen way? One makes every effort to live in a dignified and proper manner, without harming anyone else, yet people will carp and cavil and try to tear one down. It's most vexing."

He breathes a little sigh.

"Excuse me," says a small voice at his feet. "Urashima-san?"

This, of course, is our famous and problematic tortoise.

I say "problematic" because, although I don't wish to appear pedantic, I feel compelled to point out that turtles come in a great number of varieties, and that fresh-water turtles and salt-water turtles are naturally built to different specifications. The turtle we see in paintings of the goddess Benten, stretched out by the side of the pond drying its shell in the sun, is the creature I believe most of us refer to as a tortoise. And it is this same tortoise upon which in picture books we sometimes see Urashima Tarō perched, one hand shading his eyes as he peers off toward the distant Dragon Palace. But were a tortoise of this sort to dive into the ocean, it would in fact choke on the salt water and promptly expire. It is usually this type of land tortoise—and not a sea turtle or soft-shelled turtle or hawksbill—that we find, along with a crane, on those ornamental stands that represent the Isle of Eternal Youth. The crane lives a thousand years, it is said, and the tortoise ten thousand, which accounts for their presence on wedding decorations and what have you, and perhaps it's the auspicious nature of tortoises that causes illustrators of picture books to assume that Urashima-san's guide too must have been one of these (the Isle of Eternal Youth and the Dragon Palace being similar sorts of places), but one can't help but think it's a bit much to ask us to imagine a land tortoise slashing away at the water with its clumsy, clawed feet, struggling toward the bottom of the sea. No, we definitely need something along the lines of a hawksbill turtle, whose wide, fin-like appendages would permit it to glide a bit more gracefully through the deep.

I must point out, however—at the risk, once again, of appearing pedantic—that this leaves us with another thorny problem. It is my understanding that the only places in the Empire where the hawksbill turtle is found are the southern islands—Ogasawara, the Ryukyus, Taiwan, and so forth—and much as I regret to say this, it's simply not likely that a hawksbill might emerge from the Sea of Japan at a beach on the northern coast of Tango. Such being the case, and since one might argue that tales of this sort are, after all, mere flights of fancy, I considered making Urashima-san a native of Ogasawara or the Ryukyu Islands, but since ancient tradition holds that he hailed from Mizunoe, and since by all accounts an Urashima Shrine actually exists on the coast of Tango, I feel duty-bound to avoid any such indiscriminate tampering with the facts, if only out of deference for the sanctity of the Japanese historical record. No, it would appear that we must somehow impose upon a hawksbill or some other amphibious reptile of similar construction to make the long journey up through the Sea of Japan. And yet I'm reluctant to invite the scorn of persnickety zoologists who might step forward to point out the absurdity of this assertion and to denounce the appalling lack of scientific spirit displayed by irresponsible literary hacks like me.

So I gave it a little more thought. Surely, besides the hawksbill, there must be other species of sea turtle with fin-shaped appendages. Wasn't there something called a loggerhead tortoise? Once, about ten years ago (I too am getting on in years), I spent a summer at the seashore in Numazu, and I remember the fishermen there making quite a fuss about having found on the beach a sea turtle with a shell nearly five feet in diameter. I saw the thing with my own eyes and seem to recall that it was being referred to as a loggerhead tortoise. Perfect. That's the one for us. If it could crawl up on the beach at Numazu, perhaps we can, without causing too much pandemonium in zoological circles, prevail upon it to paddle around to the Sea of Japan and roll out of the surf at Tango. If, nonetheless, someone insists on raising a fuss about ocean currents being thus or such, well, don't look at me. I shall calmly reply that it is indeed strange, passing strange, that the creature should turn up in a place common sense tells us it couldn't possibly reach, and that this is proof that we're not talking about just your average loggerhead tortoise here. That so-called scientific spirit of yours is nothing to place absolute faith in, my friends. All your theorems and axioms are nothing more than conjectures in their own right, after all. You don't want to get too big for your breeches.

At any rate, this loggerhead tortoise (since the name is cumbersome and a bit of a tongue-twister, we'll refer to it simply as "the tortoise" from here on) stretches his long neck to look up at Urashima-san and say, "Excuse me, but you said a mouthful. I know just how you feel."

Urashima-san is understandably startled.

"What the . . . ? Why, you're the tortoise I rescued the other day. Don't tell me you're still loafing about on this beach?"

This tortoise, in short, is none other than the one Urashima-san discovered being tormented by a group of children, took pity on, purchased from the children, and released into the sea.

"'Loafing about'? That's cold. I'll remember that, young master. The fact is, I've been coming here every day and night since we last met, waiting for you. It seems to me I owe you a favor."

"Rather reckless of you, I'd say. Or perhaps 'rash' is the word. What if those children had found you again? Little chance you'd come out alive a second time."

"Oh, get off your high horse. I figured if I got caught, I'd just have you buy me my freedom again. Excuse me if that's rash. I needed to see you once more. It's a weakness. I'm crazy about you, young master. At least acknowledge my feelings."

Urashima smiles wryly. "Willful little thing, aren't you?"

"I beg your pardon?" the tortoise says. "Aren't you contradicting yourself, young master? Were you not just moaning about how critical people can be? Now you're calling me reckless, rash, willful. You're no slouch at criticism yourself, I see. Maybe you're the willful one. I too have my own way of living, after all. You might try to recognize that."

A stunning counterattack. Urashima blushes in spite of himself and improvises a desperate, paper-thin defense to the tortoise's poison dart. "I wasn't criticizing. I was admonishing. Offering a gentle word to the wise. 'Good advice is harsh on the ear,' as they say."

"You'd be a good sort if you weren't always putting on airs, you know that?" The tortoise sighs. "Oh, well. Enough talk. Just sit yourself down on my shell."

"What?" Urashima stares at him agog. "What a thing to say! Do you think I'm some sort of barbarian? To sit on a tortoise's shell would be— well, it would be beyond scandalous! Hardly the sort of thing for a man of refinement to do."

"Never mind all that. I just want to repay you for the favor you did me the other day. I'm going to give you a ride to the Dragon Palace. Go ahead and jump on my back."

"The Dragon Palace?" Urashima laughs. "Enough of your jokes. You've been drinking, haven't you? Of all the preposterous . . . The Dragon Palace exists only in poetry and fairy tales. It's not a real place. Do you understand? It's a dream, or an expression of yearning, you might say, that we men of refinement have indulged in since ancient times."

The attempt to come across as genteel makes him sound all the more pompous, and now it's the tortoise's turn to burst out laughing.

"You kill me. But save the lecture on refinement for later, will you? Just trust me and hop on my back. Your problem is you've never had a taste of adventure."

"Well! Now you're coming out with the same sort of impudent remarks my little sister is always making. To be sure, I am not overly fond of this 'adventure' nonsense. Adventures are rather like acrobatics. Spectacular, yes, but, in the end, boorish and worldly—a form of vice, you might almost say. Adventure has nothing to do with acceptance of one's fate, or with immersing oneself in tradition. A lover of adventure is like the proverbial blind man who fears not the snake. Someone like myself, steeped as I am in the time-honored tradition of gentlemanly refinement, cannot but hold the quest for adventure in scorn. I prefer to walk the straight, narrow, and tranquil path trod by my predecessors."

"Poo!" The tortoise explodes with laughter again. "What do you think the path of your predecessors was, but the path of adventure? Of course, 'adventure' is a poor choice of words, I suppose. You probably associate it with blood and gore and swashbuckling libertinism and heaven knows what. Let's call it, rather, 'the power to believe.' On the far side of the valley, beautiful flowers are in bloom. He who believes this won't hesitate to seek them out, though it means climbing across on slender wisteria vines. Some will call it acrobatics and applaud; others will revile the man as a show-off. But in fact that man has nothing in common with the tightrope walker at the circus. He braves those slippery vines merely because he wants to see the flowers on the other side. He's not thinking vainglorious thoughts or admiring his own adventuresome nature. It's absurd to imagine that adventure is something one might use to feed one's pride. The climber simply believes. He's convinced that there are beautiful flowers on the other side. Bystanders watch him and speak of adventure, for want of a better word. To lack a sense of adventure, then, is to lack the power to believe. Is it boorish to believe? Is it a vice?

"The problem with you men of refinement is that you actually seem to take pride in your skepticism. Skepticism isn't wisdom, young master. It's something much baser, and meaner. Miserliness, you might call it. Proof that you're obsessed with the fear of losing something. Well, relax. Nobody's after your possessions. People like you don't know how to accept the kindness of others at face value. All you can think about is what you'll have to do in return. 'Gentlemen of refinement,' my eye. Stingy bastards, is more like it."

"I beg your pardon? What a nasty thing to say! I come down to the seashore after having my younger brother and sister treat me with the utmost disrespect, only to be criticized in the same insolent manner by the tortoise whose life I recently saved! It seems to me that those who are unconcerned with their own ancestry and proud traditions tend to be unduly free with their tongues. I suppose it stems from a sort of reckless desperation. I know exactly what you're trying to do here. It's not for me to say, perhaps, but it should be obvious to the meanest intelligence that I have a loftier destiny, a higher calling, than people of your ilk. This is something that was decided at birth, and I am not to blame for it being so. It's Providence. But you people hold a grudge, and I happen to know that for all your convoluted arguments, you're really only trying to drag my destiny down to the level of your own. Mortal beings cannot alter heaven's dispensation, however. You feed me this outlandish tale about taking me to the Dragon Palace in an attempt to associate with me on equal footing, but, my dear fellow, you're wasting your breath. I know exactly what you're up to. Cease this nonsense at once and go! Swim back to the bottom of the sea, where you belong. My having gone out of my way to save you will all have been for nothing if those children catch you again. People like you don't know how to accept the kindness of others gracefully."

Undaunted by this diatribe, the tortoise laughs again.

"Ha! 'My having gone out of my way to save you'—I like that! It's a perfect example, young master, of what's so hard to stomach about you gentlemen of refinement. You think that your own acts of kindness are proof of a higher morality, and deep down inside you feel you deserve some sort of reward. But if someone shows *you* a little kindness, you're mortified. God forbid you should have to associate with someone like *me* as if we were equals, right? Ah, young master, you disappoint me! All right, then, let me put it to you straight.

"The only reason you helped me out was because I'm a tortoise and my tormentors were children. To intervene between a tortoise and children isn't likely to bring about much in the way of repercussions. What did you give them—five coppers? That's big money to a child, but it's not much skin off your back, is it? I thought you'd put up a bit more than that. Miserly isn't the word. How do you think it makes me feel? Five coppers for my life.

For you it was just a whim of the moment. 'A few coppers to rescue a tortoise—oh, hell, why not?' But suppose it wasn't children teasing a tortoise but, say, a group of rowdy fishermen tormenting some sickly beggar. Would you have offered so much as a single copper? Hardly. You would have scowled and hurried past, not wanting to get involved. Gentlemen like you despise having your faces rubbed in raw reality. I guess it makes you feel as if your lofty destiny is being dragged through the gutter.

"Kindness, for people like you, is nothing more than a minor diversion. A little titillation. You rescued me because I'm a tortoise. You put up money because they were children. But a sickly beggar and rowdy fishermen? That would be another story altogether. To have the smelly wind of real life blowing in your face would be more than you could bear. That's what we call being a snob, Urashima-san.

"Hey, you're not angry, are you? I love you, after all—or don't you want to hear that? It's a delicate situation. You people with lofty destinies seem to think it's a disgrace to be admired even by people of lowly birth, let alone a *tortoise*. To be loved by a tortoise must be repulsive to you. But, look, have a heart. Love and hate aren't based on logic, after all. It's not because you rescued me that I love you, and it's not because you're a man of refinement. I just do, that's all. And it's because I love you that I have this urge to tease you. It's how we cold-blooded creatures express our love. Well, we do have snakes in the family, so I guess I can't blame you for not trusting me. But I'm not the serpent from the Garden of Eden, for heaven's sake, I'm a genuine Japanese tortoise. I'm not scheming to entice you to the Dragon Palace so I can cause your downfall. Try to understand my feelings. I just want to play with you. I'd like us to have some fun together in a very special place.

"You won't find people disturbing the peace by criticizing one another down there. Life in the Dragon Palace is gentle, leisurely, live-and-let-live. The place is built for enjoyment. Me, I can live on land or under the sea, so I've had a chance to compare the two, and I'll tell you, life up here is too full of stress. Everyone's forever criticizing everyone else. When someone opens his mouth on land it's either to say something nasty about others or to praise himself. It gets tiresome fast. But I've been up on land like this so many times that I too have become tainted. I've learned to engage in the same sort of snobbish one-upsmanship that's so popular here. It's bad, I know, but there's something habit-forming about finding fault with others, and now life in the Dragon Palace sometimes seems dull to me. Civilization is a real monkey on my back, I'll tell you. I no longer know if I'm a creature of the sea or the land. I'm somewhere in between, I guess, like the bat—is it a bird or a beast?—and it's getting harder and harder for me to stay put in my own home. This much I can guarantee you, though: the Dragon Palace is the ultimate place to relax and have fun in. Trust me. It's a world of singing, dancing, delectable food, and wonderful wine. Perfect for a discriminating man like yourself. After all, aren't you the one who was just complaining about criticism? It doesn't exist in the Dragon Palace."

The tortoise's rather astounding garrulity is such that Urashima has given up even trying to interject a response, but these last few words pierce his heart.

"Ah," he sighs, "if only there really were such a place!"

The tortoise glares at him.

"You still doubt what I'm saying? I'm not lying to you, damn it! Now you've made me angry. Is this what all you refined gentlemen are like—wishing and pining and never acting? You make me sick."

Not even the meek and mild Urashima can back down from a challenge as pointed, and as barbed, as this.

"Very well!" he says with another wry smile. "Just as you wish. I'll climb on your back and see what happens."

But the tortoise is genuinely irate.

"The way you put things really rubs me the wrong way, you know that? What do you mean, 'and see what happens'? To climb on my back and to climb on my back *and see what happens* add up to exactly the same thing. In terms of sealing your fate, there's no difference between turning right on a whim and turning right because you've come to some momentous resolve. Either way, it can't be undone. Once you've given in to that whim, your destiny is decided. There's no such thing as 'seeing what happens' in this life. To do something just to see what happens is exactly the same as just plain doing it. You gentlemen of refinement have a lot to learn about resigning yourselves to fate. You actually think you can turn back once you've taken a leap?"

"All right! I'm climbing on your back because I believe you."

"Now you're talking!"

As Urashima seats himself on the tortoise's shell it settles and expands, until it's almost wider than he can reach across. The tortoise pushes off into the waves, rock-

ing gently from side to side. They are perhaps two stones'
throw from shore when he issues a terse command.

"Close your eyes."

Urashima obediently complies and in the next moment hears a sound like a sudden shower and feels something like a warm spring breeze, only heavier, tickling
his earlobes.

"Depth: one thousand fathoms," the tortoise an-
nounces.

Urashima experiences a slight nausea.

"Is it all right if I have to throw up?" he says, his eyes
still clamped shut.

"What? You're going to puke?" The tortoise reverts to
a coarser tone of voice as he turns his head to look back.
"What a revolting— My word! You've still got your eyes
closed, like a good little boy! That's what I love about you,
young master. You may open your eyes now. Drink in the
scenery and you'll stop feeling queasy in no time."

He opens his eyes to a vast, hazy expanse lit with an
ethereal pale green glow that casts no shadows.

"So this . . . is the Dragon Palace," he whispers dreamily.

"Snap out of it. We've only descended a thousand fathoms. The Dragon Palace is ten thousand fathoms under
the sea."

"Sheee!" Urashima's voice is a squeak. "The sea's deep,
isn't it?"

"You were raised near the sea, for heaven's sake. You sound like some ape from the mountains. Yeah, it's deep. It's not to be compared to the pond in your garden."

Ahead, behind, left, right—whichever direction Urashima looks, there is only that seemingly boundless, hazy expanse. Below him too he can see nothing but the pale green glow, and when he looks up he sees not the blue sky but an immeasurable dome of watery emerald light. Aside from their own voices, not a sound can be heard. There is only that sensation of wind, like a viscous spring breeze, blowing in his face and tickling his ears.

He finally spots something far in the distance, above and to the right—a tiny, faint, speckled something, like a handful of scattered ashes.

"What's that? A cloud?"

"You're joking, right?" says the tortoise. "There aren't any clouds in the ocean."

"What is it, then? It looks like a splash of India ink. Just dirt or something?"

"You're really showing your ignorance, you know that? It's a school of sea bream."

"Really? It looks so small from here. How many would you say there are? Two or three hundred, maybe?"

The tortoise laughs derisively. "Are you serious?"

"More, then? What, two or three thousand?"

"Get a grip on yourself, man. There are a good five or six million fish in that school."

"Five or six million? Are you joking?"

"I am, yes," the tortoise says, and grins. "It's not a school of sea bream. It's a sea fire. Awful lot of smoke, though. To make that much smoke, they must be burning an area about twenty times the size of Japan."

"Please. Fire can't burn underwater."

"Think before you speak, young master. Water contains oxygen, doesn't it? Where there's oxygen, there's no reason you can't have fire."

"Nonsense. I'm not going to fall for such half-witted sophistry. All jokes aside—what in the world is it? That little smudge up there. Is it a school of fish after all? It certainly isn't fire."

"I'm telling you, it's a fire. Haven't you ever wondered why the sea never overflows, in spite of the fact that all the rivers in the world empty into it constantly, day and night? If you look at it from the sea's point of view, it's quite a dilemma. It's not easy to manage all that surplus water rushing in. That's why we have to start these fires, to dispose of the water we don't need. Just look at it burn!"

"Don't be ridiculous. Why isn't the smoke spreading, then? What is it really? It hasn't moved at all since I've been watching, so it's not likely to be a school of fish either. Stop your teasing and tell me what it is. Please?"

"All right, all right. It's the shadow of the moon."

"You're pulling my leg again."

"No, seriously. Nothing on land casts a shadow down here, but all the heavenly bodies do, as they pass overhead. Not just the moon, but the stars and planets and everything. Down in the Dragon Palace we even have a calendar that's made by tracing those shadows. We use it

38

to determine the seasons. That moon's a little past full, so today must be, what, the thirteenth?"

The tortoise is speaking in a sincere tone of voice, and Urashima is inclined to believe him this time, but it all still seems a bit fishy somehow. He is, however, more than willing to suspend his disbelief that the one smudge on this vast pale green expanse could be the moon's shadow, if the alternative is a monstrous school of fish or, worse, smoke from a fire. For a man of cultivated tastes the moonshadow interpretation holds a good deal of charm, and he briefly entertains a certain melancholy nostalgia.

But now it begins to grow dark, and suddenly, along with an almost deafening roar, comes a rush of gale-force wind that nearly topples him from his seat.

"Better close your eyes again," the tortoise says in a no-nonsense tone. "We've just reached the entrance to the Dragon Palace. Deep-sea divers have come down this far, but they generally assume they've reached the very bottom and head back up. In fact, you're the first human being that's ever passed through here. Probably the last too."

It seems to Urashima as if the tortoise has rolled over. It's a most peculiar sensation, as though his ride has done a half-somersault and is now upside-down and swimming *upward*. He clings tightly to the shell, although he doesn't seem to be in any danger of falling off.

"You can open your eyes now."

When he does so, the sensation of being upside-down vanishes. He is sitting atop the tortoise as he has been all along, and they're still diving.

39

A dim light, as of dawn, suffuses the atmosphere around them, and Urashima can make out the vague outline of an immense row of white peaks. It appears to be a mountain range of some sort, but the peaks are so symmetrical that except for their enormous size they might be artificial structures.

"Those are mountains, right?"

"Right."

"The mountains of the Dragon Palace." Urashima's voice is hoarse with excitement.

"Right." The tortoise continues diving.

"They're pure white. Covered with snow, are they?"

"Wow. You people with lofty destinies think differently from the rest of us, you know that? I mean, it takes my breath away. You think it snows at the bottom of the sea, for example."

"Well, I'm told you have fires down here," Urashima says, in an attempt to retaliate. "So you must have snow too. Water contains oxygen, after all."

"Not much connection between snow and oxygen, I'm afraid—at least, no more than between the wind and the bucket-maker. If you're trying to bring me down a notch, you'll have to do better than that. But then, there's no reason to expect refined gentlemen to be much good at repartee, I suppose. Once you've climbed to the top, snow fun coming down—how's that? 'Sno fun, get it? Not very funny, I guess. Better than that oxygen crack, though. Oxygendeed, what? Sorry."

"Be that as it may, those mountains—"

The tortoise snorts derisively again and says, "'Be that as it may'? I love it. Be that as it may, those mountains aren't covered with snow. They're mountains of pearls."

"Pearls?" Urashima gasps. "No, you're lying. You couldn't make a mountain as high as one of those even with ten or twenty thousand pearls."

"Ten or twenty thousand? Your stinginess is showing again, young master. In the Dragon Palace we don't count pearls individually. We talk about 'hills' of pearls. Some say a hill is thirty billion pearls, but nobody's ever really bothered to count them. Put about a million hills together and you've got a mountain the size of those. We have a pearl disposal problem down here, you see. After all, if you think about it, they're just oyster poop."

As the tortoise is speaking, they reach the main entrance to the Dragon Palace. The palace gate, perched at the foot of one of the pearl mountains, emits a fluorescent glow but is surprisingly small. Urashima steps off the tortoise's back and follows behind him, stooping slightly as he passes beneath the gate's low-slung roof. Inside, it's dim and hushed.

"Awfully quiet, isn't it?" he says. "Too quiet. We aren't in Hell, are we?"

"Get a grip on yourself, young master." The tortoise slaps him on the back with a fin. "All royal palaces have this sort of hushed atmosphere. What did you imagine? Did you have some hackneyed vision of people dancing and singing and beating drums, as if it were a fishermen's festival on the beach of Tango? Don't be pathetic. I thought people like you were supposed to view quiet simplicity as the epitome of civilized taste. 'Are we in Hell?'

41

he says. Shame on you. Once you get accustomed to the silence and the subdued light, you'll be amazed to see how it comforts the heart. Watch your step, by the way. You'll cut a pretty ridiculous figure if you slip and . . . What the—? You're still wearing your sandals? Were you raised in a barn? Take them off!"

Blushing with embarrassment, Urashima hastily removes the footwear. In his bare feet, he's aware of an odd sliminess to the surface he's walking on.

"This road feels icky," he says.

"It's not a road, genius, it's a corridor. We're already inside the palace."

"We are?" Startled, Urashima looks about but can't see any walls or columns or anything of the sort. Only the dim, fathomless light wavering around him.

"Just as there's no snow down here, my friend," the tortoise says in a suddenly affectionate tone, "there's no rain either. Which means there's no need to build those horribly confining walls and ceilings and things, the way they do on land."

"But the gate had a roof."

"To make it easier to find. Princess Oto's chambers have walls and a roof as well, but that's only to protect her dignity and privacy."

"You don't say." Urashima still looks baffled. "But where are her chambers? As far as I can see, it's as lonely and desolate as Hades itself—there's not a tree or a clump of grass to be seen."

"You country boys. You see a few tall buildings and bright city lights and your mouths fall open, but you don't have the least interest in the serene, secluded beauty of a place like this. Urashima-san, that noble refinement of yours is starting to look a little suspicious. But then, I suppose it's only to be expected of a bumpkin from the wild and rocky coast of Tango. All that talk about culture and lofty destiny—it's enough to make an honest man break out in a cold sweat. And you claim to be steeped in the time-honored tradition of gentlemanly refinement—what a laugh! Here you're confronted with the real thing and you turn into a quivering hick. Well, the cat's out of the bag now. You can stop playing the gentleman."

Since arriving at the Dragon Palace, the tortoise's poison tongue has only acquired an even nastier sting. Urashima is crushed.

"But . . . but . . . I can't *see* anything!" His voice is practically a sob.

"That's why I told you to watch your step. This isn't a corridor like on land, you know. It's a bridge of fish. Hundreds of millions of fish all huddled together. Be careful."

A chill races down Urashima's spine, and he shoots to his tiptoes. No wonder the floor felt so slimy beneath his feet! Peering down, he can see that it does indeed consist of countless fish of every size and description, squeezed together gill to gill and all but motionless.

"This is horrible!" he sputters as he minces unsteadily along. "In very bad taste, I must say. Is this what you call the serene, secluded beauty of the place—having the guest walk on the backs of fish? It's the ultimate in vulgarity! Think of the poor fish, to begin with! If this is refinement, it's of a variety a bit too bizarre for simple country folk like me to comprehend!"

The opportunity to vent his resentment at having been called a hick provides a small amount of satisfaction, if only momentarily.

"Not at all, sir," says a tiny voice at his feet. "We come here each day to listen to Her Highness Princess Oto play the harp. This bridge of ours isn't an expression of refinement. We're simply entranced by the music, you see. Please feel free to walk on. We don't feel a thing, I assure you."

"Oh. I see," Urashima says with an embarrassed smile. "I thought this was meant as some sort of decorative touch to the palace environs or—"

"That's not all you thought," the tortoise interrupts. "You thought Her Highness ordered the fish to do this to give a proper welcome to the young master of—"

"See here! I did not!" Urashima protests, flustered and blushing. "Heaven knows I'm not quite so vain as all that! But, I mean, you're the one who told me that nonsense about this being the floor of the corridor, so I just, that is, I merely thought, well, I mean, the poor fish . . ."

"We don't need floors down here. I was trying to explain the fish by way of an analogy you'd be able to grasp. It seemed to me that in terms of a house on land, this would be more or less equivalent to a corridor. I wasn't just spouting nonsense. You think it hurt the fish? Here at the true bottom of the sea you weigh about as much as a sheet of paper. Haven't you noticed how light and buoyant you feel?"

Now that it's brought to Urashima's attention, he does feel rather light on his feet. But he's also acutely conscious of having been the target of a heavy stream of abuse from the tortoise, and resentment has begun to get the better of him.

"I no longer know what to believe, and it's getting harder and harder to care. This is exactly what I find so distasteful about adventure. You have no way of knowing whether you're being deceived. All you can do is trust in your guide, and if he tells you that this is that, then that's that. There's altogether too much potential for deception in this adventure business. And besides," he adds, lashing out somewhat indiscriminately now, "what's all this about a harp? I don't hear any bloody harp!"

The tortoise maintains his composure.

"You're used to surface life, where everything's on a single plane. You're still thinking north-south-east-west, but here, of course, we have two extra directions—up and down. You've been searching for Princess Oto all this time with your eyes straight ahead. An understandable error, I suppose, but why don't you look up above you? Or down below? You see, everything in the Dragon Palace is adrift. The palace gate, the fish bridge, even the pearl mountains are all shifting and moving somewhat. You don't notice because you're moving along with them—up, down, left, right. You probably think we've progressed quite some distance since we started walking, but the fact is that we're still in approximately the same place. We may even have slid backwards a bit. The way the tide is right now, it's pulling us back at a pretty good clip. We've risen too—about a hundred fathoms, I'd say.

"But let's keep going, shall we? You'll notice that the fish have started thinning out a bit. Be careful you don't step in a hole. Not that it would be all that dangerous—

you're not going to go hurtling toward the ocean floor because, as I said, you weigh about as much as a sheet of paper. And this is a bridge to nowhere, anyway. It ends just ahead, but there's nothing on the other side. Look down below you, though. *Hey, you jellyfish! Move aside there! The young master's here to see Her Highness!* These fellows form a sort of canopy over the castle proper, you see. A floating canopy of jellyfish—I should think a refined poetic sort like you would appreciate that."

The jellyfish silently part and move to either side, and now the faint plinking of a harp can be heard issuing from somewhere below. The sound is similar to that of the Japanese koto, yet not as piercing. It's a softer, more ethereal sound, with tones that seem to linger and reverberate endlessly. But what is the song? "Chrysanthemum Dew"? "The Gossamer Gown"? "Sunset"? "Ghosts"? "River of Dreams"? No, it isn't quite like any of these. The melody possesses a fragile beauty and insubstantiality that not even the genteel and poetic Urashima can define, and it resonates with a profound and noble solitude the like of which he's never heard on land.

"What a marvelous tune. What is it called?"

The tortoise listens for a moment.

"*Seitei*," he says.

"*Seitei*?"

"*Sei*—'Divine.' *Tei*—'Resignation.'"

"'Divine Resignation' . . ."

As Urashima repeats the title under his breath, he receives for the first time an intimation that life in the Dragon Palace, here at the bottom of the sea, is embued with nobility of a much higher sort than any he's ever imagined. No wonder the tortoise spoke of breaking out in a cold sweat to hear him babble about destiny and culture and the time-honored tradition of gentlemanly refinement. His refinement, he sees now, is mere imitation, mere pretense—monkey see, monkey do. He really is like some sort of mountain ape.

"From now on I'll believe every word you say. 'Divine Resignation.' Yes. Yes, of course . . ."

Urashima lingers there as if spellbound, bending his ear to that wondrous music.

"We're going to jump down from here now. Nothing dangerous about it. Just spread your arms like this and step off. You'll float down nice and easy. From here we should end up right at the foot of the stairway to the main hall. Come on, now, look alive. Ready? Follow me."

The tortoise sinks slowly out of sight. Urashima blinks as if awaking from a dream, spreads his arms, and steps off the jellyfish canopy. He's pulled gently downward, and a cool and refreshing breeze plays against his cheeks. The water turns various hues of green, rather like the dappled shade of leafy trees, the sound of the harp grows nearer and clearer, and the next thing he knows he's standing next to the tortoise at the foot of a stairway. "Stairway" is what the tortoise called it, but it's more like a gentle, unbroken slope, carpeted with countless tiny orbs that glisten with a dull, silvery sheen.

"Are these pearls too?" Urashima whispers.

The tortoise gives him a pitying look.

"You see something small and round, it must be a pearl, right? I told you the pearls get thrown away. Scoop up a handful of these and take a closer look."

Urashima bends down to gather several of the little balls in his hands. They're as cold as ice.

"Oh! It's hail!"

"Don't be stupid. Put a few of them in your mouth."

He obediently stuffs his cheeks with five or six of the cold little globes. "They're delicious!"

"Aren't they?" says the tortoise. "These are the cherries of the sea. If you eat these you'll live for three hundred years and never get any older."

"Is that right? Does it matter how many you eat?" Our refined Urashima, suddenly forgetting his manners, bends down to scoop up another handful. "I hate the idea of getting old and ugly, you know. I'm not so afraid of dying, but the ravages of age just don't match my aesthetic. I think I'll have a few more of these."

"She's *smiling*! Look up there. Her Highness has come to greet you. She looks especially lovely today."

At the top of the slope of sea cherries stands a petite young woman draped in a sheer blue gown. She's gazing down at them with a hint of a smile on her lips. Her skin, beneath the translucent gown, is as white as foam.

"Is that Princess Oto?" Urashima whispers, his face turning bright red.

"Who else would it be? Stop fidgeting, you idiot. Acknowledge her."

Urashima grows even more flustered at the suggestion.

"But what should I say? No sense in announcing my name—what does she care about someone like me? And besides, after barging in uninvited like this . . . I mean, what's the point? Let's go back."

Apparently even Urashima of the lofty destiny, when face to face with a noble and legendary princess, can turn timid and cowardly. He's ready to run.

"Her Highness has known about you for a long time. Haven't you ever heard the expression 'The palace's ears reach ten thousand leagues'? Pluck up your courage and give her a polite little bow. Besides, even if she didn't know anything about you, you wouldn't have to rack your brains like that. She's not someone who cares about personal trivialities or harbors suspicions. All you have to say is, 'I've come for a visit.'"

"Oh, sure. As if I could be so rude. Goodness, she's laughing now! I guess I'd better at least bow to her."

Urashima bows so deeply his toes are within reach of his hands.

"That's *too* polite. What's the matter with you? You're the man I owe my life to, for heaven's sake. Show a little dignity. Scraping the floor like that . . . You call yourself refined? Look—Her Highness is beckoning. Let's go. Stand straight, chest out. I want you to strut like you're the handsomest man in Japan, a man of the noblest, most refined tastes. You have no problem lording it over me with that affected attitude of yours, but face to face with a beautiful woman you turn into a quivering toad?"

"Don't be coarse. One simply cannot be too respectful of such a noble and exalted person."

Urashima is so nervous his voice is hoarse and his legs are shaking. He staggers up the slope behind the tortoise, only to find himself in a room that must measure ten thousand mats in size. Well, perhaps the word "garden" would be more appropriate. This space too is carpeted with the little hail-like cherries, shining in the leaf-green rays of light that waft through the hazy atmosphere. Here and there, in no particular arrangement, are large black rocks, the only visible objects. There is of course no roof, nor a single pillar as far as the eye can see, giving the place the air of an ancient ruin. It's some time before Urashima notices the tiny purple flowers peeping out amid the sea cherries, but these only seem to add to the solitude of the scene. He finds it amazing that anyone could bear to live in such a lonely, secluded place, and he sighs a sigh of something like wonder. Then he remembers himself and steals a glance at the princess.

Without a word, she turns her back to him and begins to walk slowly away. It's then that he notices for the first time the countless tiny golden fish, smaller than the smallest minnows, swimming along behind her: a scarcely visible, glittering golden train that conforms precisely to her every move, like an aura. She is indeed, he feels, an august being, and not of the everyday world.

Princess Oto is barefoot, her thin garment fluttering in slow motion with each step, and as Urashima watches he realizes that her small white feet are not quite touching the carpet of sea cherries. Maybe the soles of those feet have never touched anything. No doubt they're as soft and smooth as the feet of a newborn baby—a thought that only makes her unembellished body seem to him all the more exquisite, the literal embodiment of purity and no-

50

bility. He begins to feel grateful for this adventure of his, glad he allowed himself to be talked into coming to the Dragon Palace, as he dreamily follows along behind her.

"Well? Not bad, eh?" the tortoise whispers, nudging him in the ribs with a fin.

"No . . . What?" Reverie interrupted, Urashima quickly changes the subject. "These flowers, these purple flowers. They're very pretty."

"What, these things?" the tortoise says, wincing with disappointment. "They're just the flowers of the sea cherries. They look a little like violets, don't they? Sip at these petals and you'll get nice and high. They serve as our wine here. And those things that look like big rocks? They're actually algae bushes that have been growing for tens of thousands of years. They're softer and chewier than bean jam and more delicious than anything you can find on land. Each bush is a different flavor too. Down here we eat that algae, get high on the flower petals, sip the juice of the sea cherries when we're thirsty, listen to Princess Oto's harp, and watch the little fish dance about like living snow flurries. I told you when I invited you down here that it's a place of music, dance, delectable food, and wonderful wine. Is it different from what you expected?"

Urashima makes no reply but a poignant, rueful smile.

"I'll bet you expected lots of noise and commotion, trays full of sea bream and tuna sashimi, dancing girls in red kimono, stacks of damask and brocade, gold and silver and coral and—"

"Come now," says Urashima, looking somewhat insulted. "I'm not so vulgar as all that. Still, though, I've always thought of myself as a solitary sort, but after coming here and seeing a person who lives a truly lonely life I feel ashamed of the affected way I've led my own till now."

"You mean Her Highness?" The tortoise jerks his chin toward Princess Oto. "Nothing lonely about her life. She couldn't care less. It's because people have aspirations and ambitions that solitude wears on them. If you don't give a damn what the rest of the world is up to, you can be alone for a hundred years—a thousand years—with no difficulty whatsoever. At least, you can if you don't let criticism bother you. But tell me something: Where do you think you're going?"

"Hm? I'm just . . . I mean . . ." The question has caught Urashima off guard. "But you said she—"

"You think she means to give you a guided tour? Listen, she's already forgotten all about you. No doubt she's on her way back to her chambers. Snap out of it, man. This is the Dragon Palace. We're already here. There's nothing more to see. You do whatever you like here. That's not good enough for you?"

"Stop teasing me. What am I supposed to do?" Urashima is on the verge of tears again. "I mean, she came out to greet me, didn't she? It's not as if I think I'm anyone special, I just thought that following her was the proper thing to do! And I'm certainly not saying that anything's not good enough for me. You act as if I have some disgusting ulterior motive or something. You're really a nasty fellow, aren't you? I've never been teased like this before. You're quite despicable."

"And you take everything too seriously. The princess lives in her own world. You're a guest from a faraway land, and you're also the one who saved my life, so it's only natural she'd come out to greet you. Besides, you're suave, you're debonair, you're handsome . . . Wait. That part's a joke, in case you didn't know. We don't need you getting a big head again. Whenever we have unusual guests, the princess makes a point of greeting them. And after greeting them, she leaves them alone—retires to her chambers and forgets about them, so they'll feel free to do just as they please and to stay as long as they like. The truth is, not even those of us who live here ever really know what she's thinking. As I said, she's in her own world."

"Well, when you put it that way . . . I think I'm beginning to understand. Yes. Perhaps there is something in what you say. Perhaps this method of extending hospitality is in fact of the truest, noblest sort. Greet the guests and then forget about them. You leave sumptuous delicacies casually scattered about, and even the music and dance are spontaneous and unpretentious—not performed to impress anyone. Princess Oto thinks not of the listeners when she plays the harp, nor do the fish concern themselves with who might be watching as they flit about in absolute freedom. No one's anxious to be praised by the guests. And the guests, for their part, don't have to be careful about expressing their admiration. They can, if they choose, merely stretch out and pay no attention to the entertainment whatsoever. It's no breach of etiquette to merely get high and let the music carry you away.

"Yes, this is the way it should be. This is how guests ought to be received! I see that now. It's a far cry from the supposedly genteel hospitality of those small-minded schemers who press tasteless food upon their visitors, spout insincere compliments, roar with laughter at witless witticisms, feign astonishment at the most commonplace anecdotes, and exchange endless, meaningless social pleasantries. I'd love to show them how a truly magnanimous host entertains a guest. Just once I'd like them to see the treatment one gets here at the Dragon Palace! All they think of is their social standing. They tremble with fear at the thought of it slipping, and they regard their guests with wary eyes, running around in frantic circles with no more sincerity in their hearts than you could find in the last speck of dirt beneath their fingernails. 'I shall treat you to a cup of saké.' 'I shall drink to your health.' It might as well be a business contract. Disgusting!"

"That's the spirit!" the tortoise cries gleefully. "But don't get too worked up. We don't want you having a heart attack on us. Here, sit down on this algae bush and sip a few sea cherry petals. The bouquet may be a bit strong for you at first, so you might want to mix them with five or six cherries. Put them all in your mouth together and they'll melt into a cool and refreshing drink. The taste depends on the mixture. Try different combinations until you find one that suits you."

Urashima is in the mood for a rather strong drink at the moment, so he plucks three petals and places them on his tongue with a pair of cherries. In a matter of moments they dissolve into a wine so delicious that the taste alone induces a euphoric feeling that trickles pleasantly down his throat and ends as a warm glow radiating out from his belly in all directions.

"This is wonderful. The old saw expresses it exactly: 'Wine is a broom that sweeps away sorrow.'"

"Sorrow?" the tortoise presses him. "You have something to be sorrowful about?"

"Me? No. I mean, that's not what I meant." Urashima laughs to hide his embarrassment then sighs a little sigh and steals another glance at Princess Oto, who can still be seen walking slowly off in the distance. Shimmering in the wavy pale green light, she might be a rare, translucent, marvelously scented sea plant drifting away, far beyond reach. "I wonder where she's going," he mutters in spite of himself.

"I told you," the tortoise says, not quite rolling his eyes. "To her chambers, probably."

"You keep talking about chambers. Where in the world are they? I don't see a room anywhere."

Whichever way he looks there's nothing but the vast, all-encompassing greenish glow. Not so much as a hint of walls.

"Look where the princess is walking. Don't you see something beyond her, far off in the distance?"

Urashima furrows his brow and squints.

"You're right. There does seem to be something."

Perhaps a league or so away, where the sea seems as hazy and elusive as ghost tales, is a little white shape, like an underwater flower.

"Awfully small, isn't it?"

"The princess doesn't need much room to sleep by herself."

"I suppose that's true." Urashima mixes another mouthful of sea-cherry wine. "Is she always so quiet?"

"Yes. Speech blossomed from anxiety, after all. Words were fermented from the uncertainty of existence, like poisonous red mushrooms that sprout from rotting earth. It's true we have words of joy and pleasure, but aren't those the most unnatural and contrived of all? Apparently human beings experience anxiety even in the midst of joy. But in a place without anxiety there's no need for such ignoble contrivances. I've never heard Her Highness utter a single word. But, mind you, she's not like a lot of quiet people who secretly have a bitter or cynical view of things. Far from it—she hasn't a thought in her head. She just smiles that little smile, plucks at her harp, wanders about the halls, sips at the cherry petals, and generally takes things as they come. She's very easygoing."

"Oh? So she too drinks this cherry wine? It really is good stuff, isn't it? It's all a man needs. Mind if I have a bit more?"

"Help yourself. To practice self-restraint in a place like this would be the height of idiocy. You have unlimited license here. Why don't you eat something as well? Every algae bush you see is a rare delicacy. You want something substantial? Or something light and tart? Any flavor you like, we've got it."

"I can hear the harp again. I suppose it's all right to lie down and listen awhile."

Unlimited license. This is something Urashima has never before experienced. Forgetting all about his refinement—and everything else, for that matter—he sprawls out on his back. "Ahh . . . It feels good to get high and just stretch out like this. Wouldn't mind nibbling on something while I'm at it. Is there any algae here that tastes like roasted pheasant?"

"There is," says the tortoise.

"And, let's see, how about mulberries?"

"I suppose you can find that flavor too. But I must say you've got awfully provincial tastes."

"Just revealing my true colors. I'm only a hick from the sticks, y'know." Even his manner of speaking has changed.

Looking up, he can see a misty blue dome made of schools of countless fish serenely revolving high above him; and even as he watches, one school breaks away from the others and swiftly scatters in every direction, silvery scales glinting and swirling like snow in a raging blizzard.

In the Dragon Palace there is no day or night. It's like a perpetual morning in May, cool and fresh and suffused with leafy green rays of light. Urashima has no idea how long he's been here now, but he has indeed been granted unlimited license during his stay. He has even visited Princess Oto's chambers. She displays not the slightest aversion, but merely smiles her faint, ambiguous smile.

A time comes, however, when Urashima has had his fill. Perhaps he's grown bored with absolute freedom. He begins to miss his modest life on land and to think of those who remain there, fretting over their mutual criticisms, weeping with sorrow and rage, furtively living out their meager lives, as charming and somehow very beautiful.

He goes to Princess Oto and bids her farewell. Even this sudden departure of his is met with only a wordless smile of acquiescence. Nothing is unacceptable. He's been given unlimited license from the very beginning of his stay until the very end. Princess Oto comes as far as the great stairway to see him off and silently hands him a seashell. It's a tightly closed bivalve shell of five brilliant colors. This is, of course, the famous "jeweled box" that Urashima carries home with him.

Once you've climbed to the top, 'sno fun coming down. In a kind of daze he settles on the tortoise's back again and leaves the palace behind. A strange sort of melancholy wells up in his breast. *Ah*! he thinks, *I forgot to say thank you! There's nowhere in the world to match that place! I should have stayed forever!* But he knows he's a creature of the land. No matter how easy life may have been in the Dragon Palace, his own home, his old hometown, would forever be on his mind. Even when drinking that wonderful wine, his dreams were always of home.

It saddens him to admit it, but he knows he isn't worthy of living a life of ease in that wonderful palace.

"Ngah! This won't do! I feel so lonesome!" Urashima croaks with something very close to despair. "Tortoise! Let me hear some of those spirited wisecracks of yours! You haven't said a word since we left." Which is true. The tortoise has been silently flapping his fins and forging doggedly ahead. "Are you angry? Angry because I'm leaving so suddenly, like a guest who eats and runs?"

"Don't be neurotic. This is what I hate about you land-lubbers. You want to leave, you leave. How many times have I told you that, from the very beginning? Anything you want to do is fine."

"You do seem rather down in the mouth, though."

"Look who's talking. As for me, well, I don't mind welcoming people, but seeing them off just isn't my cup of tea."

"'Sno fun, eh?"

"'Sno time for bad puns. I'll tell you, though, I never could get enthusiastic about these send-offs. All I can do is sigh, and anything I think of to say sounds so empty. I just want to get to goodbye and get it over with."

"So you feel sad too?" Urashima is touched. "Well, allow me to express my gratitude for all you've done for me. I mean that."

The tortoise doesn't reply but jiggles his shell as if to brush off the sentiment and continues paddling onward and upward.

"I guess she's back down there now amusing herself all alone." A disconsolate sigh escapes Urashima's lips. "She gave me this beautiful shell. It's not something to eat, is it?"

The tortoise guffaws.

"It didn't take you long down there to become a real pig, did it? No, the shell isn't for eating. There may be something inside it. I'm not sure."

Let us pause here for a moment. It would be easy to interpret the tortoise's casual remark as a sinister appeal to human curiosity, made much in the spirit of the serpent of Eden. Perhaps, one thinks, it is simply the nature of cold-blooded creatures to pull such tricks. But no. To see the tortoise's words in this way would be to do the good fellow a great disservice. Didn't he himself once insist that he was "a genuine Japanese tortoise" and not to be compared with the serpent in the Garden? What reason have we to disbelieve him? Judging from his attitude toward Urashima up to this point, one must conclude that the tortoise scarcely seems the sort to whisper seductively while secretly plotting destruction. In fact, he seems quite the opposite of a deceptive schemer—he is, rather, as open as a carp streamer in the winds of May. In other words, he harbors no evil intentions. So I, at least, prefer to believe.

"But you might be better off not opening that shell," he goes on. "It's likely to contain, at the very least, the spirit energy of the Dragon Palace. Released on land, it could induce strange, mirage-like visions—or even madness. Then again, for all I know, the tides might rise in a surge and flood the earth. Let's just say that I don't think anything good could come of releasing whatever's inside."

There's no nonsense in the tortoise's voice, and Urashima is convinced of his sincerity.

"Perhaps you're right. In any case, the noble atmosphere of the Dragon Palace could only be defiled by the coarse and brutish air of earth. It might even cause an explosion of some sort. I'll store the shell at home, unopened, and treasure it as a family heirloom."

They've now reached the surface of the sea. The sunlight is blindingly bright, but Urashima can see the beach of his old hometown. He can scarcely wait to run home, call his mother and father and sister and brother and all the servants together, and regale them with a detailed account of his visit to the Dragon Palace, filling them in on all his newly acquired knowledge. *Adventure is the power to believe. The customs of this world are just mean-spirited games of Monkey See, Monkey Do. Orthodoxy is merely an-*

other name for the commonplace. The ultimate refinement is the state of Divine Resignation, which is by no means to be confused with just giving up. There's no caviling criticism in the Dragon Palace, only an eternal smile of acceptance. You're given unlimited license. Do you understand? The guest is completely forgotten about! Ah, how could you understand? And if that stark realist of a brother of his displays even a hint of disbelief, all Urashima will have to do to squelch him is to thrust that beautiful souvenir from the palace in front of his nose.

He's so worked up that as soon as they reach shore he leaps from the tortoise's back and runs for home, forgetting even to bid his ride farewell, but . . .

What happened to the village?
What happened to the house?
Nothing to see but empty fields.
No people! No roads!
And the only sound was the wind in the pines.

That's how the story goes. After much bewilderment and despair, Urashima decides to pry open the shell. But, again, I don't feel that the tortoise bears any responsibility for that. This weakness of human beings—the psychology that makes us particularly curious about what's inside something we're told we mustn't open—is also treated in Greek mythology, with the story of Pandora's box. But Pandora was the victim of a revenge scheme cooked up by the gods. They announced a prohibition on opening the box because they craftily foresaw that her curiosity would get the better of her. Our good tortoise, on the other hand, was simply being considerate when he warned Urashima. I think it's safe to trust him on this, if only because he uttered his warning with such uncharacteristic earnestness. The tortoise was an honest fellow.

But, although I can confidently attest that the tortoise is not to blame, we're left with another baffling question. When Urashima opens his gift, white smoke rises up from inside and he himself is instantly transformed into a three-hundred-year-old man. And that's how the story ends: he shouldn't have opened the shell after all—just look what happened to the poor fellow! I, however, am deeply suspicious of this ending. Does it not imply that Princess Oto's gift was a device for exacting revenge or meting out punishment, just like Pandora's box? Did the princess—even as she smiled in noble silence and granted unlimited license—secretly harbor a dark, sadistic side and a desire to punish Urashima for his selfish ways? Surely not, but why then would Princess Oto, the ultimate in refinement, give her guest such an incomprehensible gift?

From Pandora's box, all the malign hobgoblins known to man—disease, fear, enmity, grief, suspicion, jealousy, wrath, hatred, execration, impatience, remorse, cravenness, avarice, sloth, violence, and what have you—arose in a swarm like flying ants and dispersed to lodge and thrive in every corner of the earth. But when Pandora hung her head, aghast at what she'd done, it's said that she discovered, stuck to the bottom of the box, a tiny, starlike jewel. And written on the jewel was, of all things, the word "hope." At this, it's said, a hint of color returned to Pandora's pallid cheeks. And ever since then, thanks to this "hope," human beings have been able to summon the courage to endure the tribulations visited upon them by the aforementioned hobgoblins.

Compared to such a box, Urashima's souvenir of the Dragon Palace has no charm or appeal whatsoever. All it contains is smoke and an instant ticket to extreme old age. Even if a tiny star of hope had remained at the bottom of the seashell, Urashima was now three hundred years old. To give hope to a tercentenarian would be little more than a cruel joke. Hope is useless to him now. How about slipping him a little of that Divine Resignation? Then again, any man three centuries old is going to be resigned already, whether or not you bestow such an affected keepsake upon him. In the end, there's nothing you can do to mitigate what has happened. No way to save Urashima. Look at it any way you like, this would seem to have been a singularly ghastly gift. But we can't just throw in the sponge here. What if Westerners were to get wind of this and run around claiming that Japan's fairy tales are more brutal or gruesome than their darling Greek myths? That would be too mortifying for words. In order to avoid dishonoring the fabled Dragon Palace, therefore, I am determined to find an exalted meaning behind that puzzling gift.

It may be true that a few days in the Dragon Palace are equivalent to a few centuries on land, but why was it necessary to bundle up all the time that had dripped past and give it to Urashima to carry home with him? If he had simply been transformed into a white-haired old man the moment he set foot on land, one could appreciate the logic. But if, in her mercy, Princess Oto had wanted Urashima to remain a young man forever, why go to the trouble of giving him a gift too volatile to be opened? She could have just kept the shell in some dark corner of the palace. It was like asking a guest to cart away all the urine and feces he'd excreted during his visit—a spiteful and ugly thing to do. No, it was impossible for me to imagine Princess Oto, with her smile of Divine Resignation, scheming against her man like some battle-axe from the tenements. I just didn't get it. I pondered this issue for a long time, and only recently do I feel that I've begun to understand. Our mistake is that we consider what happened to Urashima to have been a tragedy, a great misfortune. But not even the picture books, when depicting the three-hundred-year-old Tarō, show him looking terribly unhappy.

**In the blink of an eye,
he became a white-haired old man.**

That's how it ends. We worldly folk, on hearing this, are the ones who blindly pass judgment. "The poor fellow!" we say, or perhaps, "What a fool!" But for Urashima, suddenly becoming three hundred years old was most decidedly *not* a misfortune. Had he found salvation in a tiny star of hope, I must say that it would have seemed to me a childish and artificial ending. Urashima was saved by the transformative puff of smoke itself. There's no need for anything to be stuck to the bottom of the shell. Allow me to put it this way:

Time and tide are man's salvation.

Oblivion is man's salvation.

It's possible to view Princess Oto's gift as the ultimate expression of the Dragon Palace's exquisite and noble hospitality. Isn't it said that memories only grow more beautiful with time? As for the unleashing of those three hundred years, that too had been entrusted to Urashima's own emotional state. He was being granted unlimited license even now that he was back on land. If he hadn't despaired, he wouldn't have turned to the shell. It was only to be opened if he simply couldn't think of anything else to do. Once it was opened, *poof!*—three hundred years and instant oblivion. I won't belabor the point any further. This is the sort of profound compassion that permeates Japanese fairy tales.

It's said that Urashima Tarō lived another ten years as a happy old man.

Click-Clack Mountain

The rabbit in the story of Click-Clack Mountain is a young female, and the tanuki badger she so thoroughly destroys is an unattractive male who's madly in love with her. There's no doubt in my mind that these are the true facts of the case.

The incident is said to have occurred in the province of Kōshū, in the hills behind what is now the town of Funazu, on the shore of Lake Kawaguchi (one of the Five Lakes of Mount Fuji). There is a rowdy, rough-and-ready side to human nature in Kōshū, and perhaps that's why this tale is somewhat more hard-boiled than other Japanese children's stories. It's steeped in cruelty right from the start. I mean, "grandmother stew"? It's downright gruesome. There's no way to make an outrage like that seem comical or witty. Let's face it: the tanuki pulled a monstrous trick. Once we find out that the old woman's bones have been scattered beneath the floorboards, we know we've entered a realm of grisliest darkness.

As so-called children's literature, therefore, I'm afraid the original tale must accept its current ignominious fate of being banned from sale. Contemporary picture books

of *Click-Clack Mountain* seem, wisely, to leave it at the tanuki merely injuring Obā-san and fleeing. That prevents
the books being banned, which is all well and good, but
now the revenge the rabbit exacts upon the tanuki seems
excessive; and, in any case, the rabbit's methods have
nothing in common with the noble tradition of cutting
down one's enemy in a gallant and straightforward manner. No, it's burn him half to death, torment and tease
him, and finally send him gurgling to the lake bottom in
a dissolving boat of mud. It's all about deception, from
start to finish. This is hardly a technique sanctioned by
Bushidō, our nation's Way of the Warrior. If the tanuki
has actually tricked Ojī-san into eating a stew containing
the flesh of his own murdered wife, then he is guilty of a
loathsome crime and we are less outraged at the torture
to which he is subsequently subjected. But to have the
tanuki merely injure the old woman—albeit out of con-
sideration for the effect on impressionable young minds,
not to mention the fear of being banned from sale—is to
make the pain and humiliation meted out to him, culmi-
nating in that inglorious death by drowning, seem more
than a bit unjust.

This tanuki badger had been living a leisurely life in
the mountains, a mischievous but fundamentally harmless moocher and ne'er-do-well, when he was captured by
the old man. Facing a hopeless situation and on the verge
of being made into tanuki stew, he writhed in agony as
he racked his brains for a way out and at last resorted to
tricking the old woman in order to save his own skin.
Let us be clear: there can be no excuse for the heinous
grandmother stew scheme, and no punishment could be
too severe for its perpetrator. But if the tanuki merely

scratched the old woman, injuring her, as in the picture books nowadays, the sin seems far less unforgivable. The tanuki, after all, was fighting for his life and so focused on what might be called justifiable self-defense that perhaps he injured the old woman without even intending to do so. I was in the bomb shelter reading *Click–Clack Mountain*, the picture book, to our five-year-old daughter, who has the misfortune of resembling her father not only physically but intellectually, when, to my surprise, she said, "The poor tanuki!"

Granted, this use of the adjective "poor" is something she's learned just recently and uses quite indiscriminately. Poor this, poor little that. On this particular occasion, she was using it as a transparent ploy to affirm an emotional bond with her sentimental pushover of a mother. Furthermore, it's possible that, on accompanying her father to the nearby Inokashira Zoo recently and seeing the band of tanuki badgers bustling tirelessly about in their cage there, the child had become convinced that these creatures are worthy objects of our affection. It may be that her sympathy for the tanuki in *Click–Clack Mountain* was based on nothing more complicated than that. In any case, the judgment of a pint-sized partisan in my household is nothing we need take too seriously. Her reasoning lacks solid foundation. The impetus behind her sympathy is unclear and her opinion therefore scarcely deserving of our attention. Irresponsible though her remark may have been, however, I couldn't help but think she had a point. The rabbit's revenge was too extreme. One can always somehow explain it away to a child this small, but wouldn't an older child, already educated in the ethics of Bushidō and the square fight, consider the rabbit's methods "dirty," to say the least? *Hmm*, the fool of a father says to himself and furrows his brow. *This is a serious problem.*

Any child in national primary school would surely sense something wrong with a plotline in which the tanuki is subjected to such a tragic and horrible undoing for the minor crime of scratching an old woman (as the picture books nowadays have it). The rabbit toys with him sadistically, sets fire to his hide, slathers red hot pepper paste on the burns, and finally fools him into boarding a boat made of mud and sailing to a watery grave. But even if the tanuki was guilty of the heinous grandmother stew plot—let alone a mere clawing incident—why not confront him openly? Why not declare your name and grievance and cut him down with a righteous sword?

The fact that rabbits are physically unimposing is no excuse. All vendettas must be carried out openly, whatever the odds. God is on the side of justice. Even if you have no chance of winning, you must attack head on, calling out for divine assistance! If you're weaker than the enemy, then you must toughen up: expose yourself to hardship and privation by going somewhere remote like Mount Kurama and training assiduously in swordsmanship and all that sort of thing. Most of the great Japanese heroes of the past did something along those lines. There seem to be, on the other hand, no other revenge tales in our nation in which, whatever the provocation, deceptive wiles are employed to worry the enemy to death. In short, there's something unsavory about the vendetta portrayed in *Click-Clack Mountain*. It's not the least bit manly in nature, and any child, or any adult—anyone who aspires to justice—must surely experience a certain discomfort when hearing the tale.

But never fear. I gave this a lot of thought, and the answer is clear to me now. It's only natural that there was nothing manly about the rabbit's way of doing things, because *the rabbit wasn't a man.* This is definitive; there can be no question about it. The rabbit was a sixteen-year-old maiden. Nothing sexual about her yet, but a real beauty. And it is precisely this sort of woman that is the cruelest of human types. In Greek myths there are a number of beautiful goddesses, but apparently the virgin goddess Artemis was considered, aside from Aphrodite, the most attractive. As you probably know, Artemis was a lunar goddess, and a shiny, silver-white crescent moon adorned her forehead. She was agile and headstrong—a sort of female version of Apollo—and all the fearsome wild beasts of the earth were her vassals. But by no means was she one of those big, tough, rawboned females. She was, rather, a vixenish little thing, petite and slender, with lithe, graceful limbs. Though she was small-breasted and lacked the voluptuous "womanliness" of Aphrodite, her face was so bewitchingly pretty it could give you the chills. But Artemis thought nothing of doing the cruelest things to anyone who displeased her. She once angrily splashed water on a man who surprised her while bathing, thereby turning him into an antlered stag. That was for catching a glimpse of her in the nude–imagine if you tried holding her hand! Any man who fell in love with a woman like this would be sure to suffer unendurable humiliation. And yet men, particularly men of negligible intelligence, are often drawn to such dangerous types. The result is always fairly predictable.

Anyone who doubts this need only observe our poor tanuki. He's been secretly in love with his "Bunny" for some time. Knowing as we do that the rabbit is a young female of the Artemis type, we can only nod deeply and sigh. Typical of men who fall in love with Artemisians, the tanuki cuts a sorry figure even among his peers. He's a dimwitted, gluttonous boor, and the forthcoming tragedy is, sadly, all too predictable.

The tanuki, trapped by Ojī-san and about to be made into tanuki stew, struggles for his life, desperate to see his beloved Bunny once again, and escapes to the mountain, where he walks about muttering to himself as he searches for her. Finally their paths cross.

"Be glad for me!" he barks proudly. "I just came *this close* to dying! While the old man was away, I gave the old woman what for and ran like hell. I'm a lucky fellow, I tell you," he says, and describes in detail his brush with disaster, punctuating the story with flying spit. The rabbit hops back a step to dodge the precipitation and shoots him a disdainful look.

"Say it, don't spray it! Disgusting. And why should I be glad? Ojī-san and Obā-san are my friends. Didn't you know that?"

"Really?" The tanuki droops. "I didn't realize. Forgive me. If I'd known they were your friends, I'd have gone ahead and let them make me into tanuki stew, or whatever they wanted!"

"It's a little late for that now. What a terrible liar you are, though, saying you didn't know! I know you know that I play in their yard sometimes, and that sometimes they give me those soft, yummy beans to eat. Well, from this moment on consider me your mortal enemy." Cold words, but the seeds of vengeance are already germinating in the rabbit's heart. A maiden's fury is bitter to the root. She knows no mercy, particularly for the ugly and stupid.

"Forgive me! I really didn't know! I'm not a liar! Please believe me!" The tanuki pleads and whines, his neck extending as his head hangs low. He spots a nut lying at his feet, plucks it from the ground and pops it into his mouth. His eyes dart about in search of others as he continues: "I mean, when you get mad at me like this, I swear, I just want to die."

"Listen to you. All you ever think about is eating!" The rabbit lifts her nose and turns away with a great display of scorn. "You're not only a filthy pig, you're a voracious pig!"

"Please don't judge me for my hunger!" He takes a step forward, still searching the ground for fallen nuts. "I wish I could make you understand how I'm suffering inside."

"I told you not to get so close to me. You smell bad. Step back. They say you ate a lizard. That's right, I heard all about it. And then—what a scream!—someone said you ate a piece of poop!"

"That's ridiculous!" The tanuki grins sheepishly. For whatever reason, however, he seems unable to deny the accusation with any vehemence, merely twisting his lips and feebly repeating, "Ridiculous."

"You're not fooling anyone. The stink of you tells the story."

No sooner has she delivered this stunning blow than the rabbit suddenly lights up as if a wonderful thought has just occurred to her. She turns to the tanuki with shining eyes and what looks like a suppressed smile.

"Well, all right. I'll forgive you, just this once. Whoa— I told you to stand back! Can't take my eye off you for two seconds. How about wiping that drool? Your jowls are soaked with it. Now calm down and listen. I'll forgive you this one time, but there's a condition. Ojī-san is terribly dispirited right now, you know. He doesn't even have the energy to go to the mountains to gather firewood. So let's gather some for him."

"You and me? Together?" Glimmerings of hope flicker in the tanuki's small, cloudy eyes.

"You don't want to?"

"'Don't want to'? Are you kidding me? We can go to-day—right now!" His voice is hoarse with ecstasy.

"Let's make it tomorrow, all right? Early morning. You've been through a lot today, and I suppose you could use a meal and some rest." Her tone is eerily compassionate.

"Oh, I appreciate that! Tomorrow I'll make a big box lunch to take, and we'll go, and I'll work with total and complete single-minded devotion, and I'll cut a whole bushel of firewood and deliver it to Ojī-san's house! If I do that, you'll forgive me, right? You'll be friends with me, right?"

"Suddenly *you're* laying down conditions? Well, it all depends on your results, of course. Maybe we could become friends."

"Eh, heh, heh!" The tanuki leers, suddenly displaying his lecherous side. "That's a coy way to put it. She's sly, this one. I'm just—" he starts to say but pauses to snag a passing spider with his tongue and slurp it down. "I'm just so happy. I almost feel like crying."

He rubs his nose and pretends to wipe a tear.

It's a brisk, invigorating summer morning. The surface of Lake Kawaguchi is shrouded in smoky white mist. Up on the mountainside, the tanuki and the rabbit are drenched in that mist as they toil away cutting and bundling sticks.

The tanuki displays not the single-minded devotion he promised, so much as a mindless frenzy, and it makes for a disturbing sight. Groaning exaggeratedly—*Unngh! Unngh!*—he swings his sickle with reckless abandon, letting out occasional howls of pain. He dashes left and right and back and forth in his fanatical quest for dead sticks, clearly wanting only to show his beloved Bunny what a hard worker he is. It isn't long, of course, before he runs out of steam. Wearing a look of utter exhaustion, he tosses the sickle aside.

"Look at this. Look at all the blisters on my hands. Ooh . . . They hurt. And I'm so thirsty! Hungry too. I mean, that was some serious manual labor I just did. Let's take a little break, what? Open up the old box lunch, and . . . oof, foo, foo!" Laughing this odd-sounding, embarrassed laugh, he reaches for the lunch box, which is about the size of a large oilcan, opens it, sticks his nose inside, and begins slurping up the contents. This he does with genuine single-minded devotion, not to mention sound effects: *mush-mush, gatz-gatz, pep-pech.* The rabbit looks up from her work and gapes at him, aghast. She sidles over to look inside the container but immediately draws back, giving a little cry of horror and covering her face with both hands. It seems there are some rather extraordinary ingredients in that lunch.

But today, for reasons of her own, the rabbit isn't heaping the usual abuse on the tanuki. She has remained silent all morning, wearing a manufactured half-smile on her lips, efficiently gathering firewood, and ignoring the overly excited tanuki's manic behavior. Even after viewing the contents of the lunch and receiving a serious shock, she neither complains nor gags but goes right back to cutting wood. She's downright tolerant today, and the tanuki is very pleased with himself: *Is she finally falling for me, after seeing the way I cut firewood? Well, what woman wouldn't be impressed by a muscular performance like that? Some lunch, though—I'm stuffed! Kinda sleepy too. Maybe a little nap . . .* Convinced he's earned a bit of self-indulgence, he stretches out and is soon snoring loudly. Whatever fool dreams he's dreaming, he holds forth at some length in his sleep— "Love potions don't work, I tell ya!"—and doesn't awake until nearly noon.

"You slept a long time," the rabbit says gently. "I've tied my firewood into one big bundle. You do the same, and we'll carry it all down to Ojī-san's house."

"Let's do that, yeah." The tanuki yawns extravagantly, scratching his arm. "I'm starving. It's not good for me to be sleeping the day away on an empty stomach," he says, and gravely adds, "I'm sensitive, you know. All right, then, I'll hurry up and bundle all that wood I cut. The lunch box is empty, after all. Time to wrap this up and find some food."

They head back down the mountain, both bearing large bundles of sticks strapped to their backs.

"You go first," says the rabbit. "I'm afraid there might be snakes around here."

"Snakes? *I'm* not afraid of no snakes. If I see any, I'll just catch 'em and—" He's about to say *eat 'em* but swallows the words. "I'll catch 'em and kill 'em. Just follow me."

"It's so nice to have a big, strong man around at times like this."

"You flatter me," the tanuki says, puffing out his chest. "But, really, you're being awfully sweet today. *Too* sweet, almost. You're not going to take me back to Ojī-san's and have him make me into tanuki stew, are you? Ah, ha, ha, ha! Anything but that!"

"Well, if you're so suspicious, you needn't bother coming. I'll go alone."

"No! I didn't mean it like that. I'll go with you. It's just . . . I'm not afraid of snakes, or anything else in this world, but that Ojī-san is a tough customer. I mean, he was going to eat me for dinner! Pretty barbaric, if you ask me. At least, it's not exactly what you'd call *genteel*. Tell you what—I'll carry this wood as far as the big hackberry tree just short of his yard, and you take it from there, all right? That's as far as I go. I mean, if I came face to face with old Ojī-san right now, I wouldn't know what to say. It'd just be awkward. Hey, what's that? I hear something. What do you think it is? Hear it? It's like a *click, clack* sound."

77

"Well, what do you expect? This is Click-Clack Mountain."

"Click-Clack Mountain? This one we're on?"

"Yes. Didn't you know that?"

"Nope. I never knew this mountain *had* a name. Pretty weird name too. You're kidding me, right?"

"Heavens, no! All mountains have names, you know—Mount Fuji, Mount Nagao, Ōmuro Mountain. This one's named after the sound it makes. There it goes again, hear it? *Click, clack.*"

"I hear it all right. Funny, though. I never heard it before, not even once. I was born on this mountain and in thirty-some-odd years here, I—"

"My! Is that how old you are? The other day you told me you were seventeen! You beast. I *thought* your face was too wrinkled and your back too bent for seventeen, but I didn't think you'd try to shave off twenty whole years! You must be almost forty, right? That's *old*."

"No, no! Seventeen. I *am* seventeen. Seventeen. Hey, sometimes my back might look a little bent when I walk, but it's not because of age. It's just a natural reaction to hunger. When I said 'thirty-odd-years,' I was talking about my brother. My brother is always using that expression, see, and I just sort of picked it up. Expressions can be contagious, right? You know how it is, kid."

He's so flustered that he's gone and called her "kid."

"I see." The rabbit remains cool. "But I never knew you had an older brother. In fact, I remember you saying, 'Oh, I'm so lonely, I'm so alone, I have no parents or brothers or sisters.' Those were your exact words. You told me I had no idea what it felt like to be all on your own. So?"

"Right. That's right." Not even the tanuki knows what he's trying to say now. "That's why everything is so complicated in this world. Nothing is black or white. Sometimes you might have a brother and sometimes you might not."

"That doesn't even make any sense," the rabbit says disparagingly. "It's just crazy talk."

"Yeah, no, the truth is, I do have one brother. I hate even to say it, but he's a drunkard and a layabout and just a complete embarrassment, and I'm really ashamed of him, but for thirty-some-odd years—I'm talking about my brother now—he's been a burden to me. Ever since he was born."

"That doesn't make sense either. How can a seventeen-year-old carry a burden for thirty-some-odd years?"

The tanuki pretends not to hear this.

"There are a lot of things in this world that can't be explained easily. At any rate, I disowned him long ago. He's dead to me. Hey, what's that? I smell something burning. Do you smell it?"

"No."

"No?" Since the tanuki is always eating noisome things, he has little confidence in own nose. He tilts his head, a puzzled look on his face. "Is it just me? Hey, now it sounds like wood burning. *Crackle-crackle, burn-burn.* You hear that?"

"What do you expect? This is Crackle-Burn Mountain."

"Don't give me that. You just said it was called Click-Clack Mountain."

"That's right. The same mountain can have different names, depending on the location. On the slope of Mount Fuji is a big bump called Little Fuji, and Ōmuro Mountain and Mount Nagao are almost like parts of Fuji too. Didn't you know that?"

"No, I did not. I've been here on this mountain for thirty-some-odd— I mean, according to my brother, they've always just called this the Mountain in Back. Phew! It's getting awfully warm. This is a weird day. What's next? An earthquake? Wow, it's hot. Whoa! Hey! Ow, ow, ow! Damn! Help! The firewood's burning! Owwwww!"

The next day, the tanuki is in his hole moaning and groaning.

"Oh, the pain! Is this the end? I must be the unluckiest man who ever lived. Just because I was born a bit better-looking than most, the women are afraid to approach me. A man who looks dapper and sophisticated is at a real disadvantage, I tell you. They probably take me for a woman-hater. Hell, I'm no saint. I like women. But they all seem to think I'm some sort of high-minded idealist and never try to seduce me. It's enough to make me run in circles, tearing my hair out and screaming, 'I love women!' Ouch! These burns are no joke. Sting like hell. Just when I thought I'd escaped the tanuki stew fate, my luck runs out on Burncrackle Mountain or whatever it was. Stupid mountain. The firewood bursts into flames while it's still on your back. Horrible place. Thirty-some-odd—" he starts to say, then looks around, as if to make sure no one is listening. "Hell, what've I got to hide? I'm thirty-seven this year. Ahem. What of it? In three more years I'll be forty. I know that. It's only natural, the natural course of nature, any—ouch!—body can see that. From the time I was born thirty-seven years ago I've lived and played on the Mountain in Back, but I've never had a weird experience like that before. Click-Clack Mountain, Crackle-Burn Mountain—even the names are strange. Something mysterious about it all."

He racks his brain for answers, beating his own head with his fists, and only stops pummeling himself when he hears the voice of a medicine peddler outside.

"Wizard's Gold Ointment! Get your Wizard's Gold Ointment! Is anyone suffering from burns, cuts, or a swarthy complexion?"

More than burns, it's the last-named affliction that catches the tanuki's attention.

"Hey, Wizard's Gold!"

"Who calls, and how may I help you?"

"Over here. In the hole. It really works on the complexion?"

"Within a single day, sir."

"Woo-hoo!" He crawls out of the hole, clambers to his feet, and freezes. "Hey! You're the rabbit!"

"I am indeed a rabbit, sir, but I'm a male rabbit and a medicine peddler. Yes, for thirty-some-odd years I've traveled this region, peddling medicine."

"Phew," the tanuki sighs and tilts his head. "You sure look like that other rabbit, though. Thirty-some-odd

81

years, eh? Well, let's not talk about the passage of time. So boring! I mean, enough is enough. And there you have it." Having wrapped up this incoherent digression, he jumps to the point. "Say, how about giving me a taste of that medicine? Truth is, I've got a little condition, you see, and—"

"My! Those are terrible burns you've got there, sir. They must be treated. If not, you'll surely die."

"Well, I'm just about *ready* to die, I'll tell you. And I don't care about the damn burns. The truth is, well, right now, I was thinking more about, you know, my skin color, because—"

"I beg your pardon, sir? This a matter of life and death! The most severe burns are on your back, I see. How in the world did this happen?"

"Well, I'll tell you," the tanuki says with a grimace. "Just because I walked down some hill with the fancy name of Crackle-Burn Mountain, all these crazy things started happening. I was as surprised as anybody."

The rabbit snickers in spite of herself. The tanuki can't see the joke but laughs along anyway.

"Ah, ha, ha, ha! Crazy, crazy things, I tell you. Let me give you some advice, pal. Don't go near that mountain. First you're on Click-Clack Mountain, and then it becomes Crackle-Burn Mountain, and that's where it goes bad. Terrible things happen. You're best off just stopping at Click-Clack. Stray on to Crackle-Burn, and—well, you see what can happen. Ow! You listening? Let this be a warning to you. You're still a young fellow, I see, but that's no reason to laugh at your seniors—I mean, not that I'm

82

old, but—let's just say you need to respect what your more experienced pals tell you. Ow."

"Thank you, sir, I'll be careful. And to express my gratitude for your kind advice, I won't charge you for the medicine. Please allow me to put some on those burns on your back. It's a good thing I happened along. You might well have died from these burns. Maybe it's a sort of divine guidance that brought me here. We must have some kind of connection, you and I."

"Maybe so," the tanuki says huskily. "Well, as long as it's free, slap it on. I'm flat broke these days. I'll tell you, fall in love with a woman and you end up spending a lot of cash. Put a drop of that medicine on my hand too, would you?"

"To what end, sir?"

"What? No, no reason. I just want to, you know, look at it—see what color it is and everything."

"It looks like any other medicine. See?" The rabbit allows a pea-size drop to drip on the tanuki's outthrust palm and is startled to see him immediately attempt to smear it on his face. She knows that if he does that, the true nature of the medicine will be revealed to him before it's done its job, so she grabs hold of his wrist. "Don't put it on your face! This medicine is too strong for that. It's dangerous!"

"Let go of me!" the tanuki squeals. "Please let go, I beg you! You don't understand. You don't know how it feels, you don't know the heartbreaking experiences this skin color has caused me in my thirty-odd years. Let go. Let go of my wrist! Please!"

The tanuki finally gives the rabbit a swift kick, breaking loose, then smears the ointment on his face with such speed that his hand is a mere blur.

"The thing about my face is, my features—my eyes and nose and everything—aren't bad. I mean, not bad at all, if I do say so myself, but even so I always felt inferior, see, just because I'm a little darker than most. So if this could fix that . . . Wait. Wow! That's too much. It stings! That's some strong medicine, all right. Then again, I have a feeling it's *got* to be strong to whiten *my* skin. Whoa. Too much. I can take it, though. Hell, next time she sees me she'll gaze at my face, all dreamy-eyed, and—woo, hoo, hoo!—I'll tell you what, don't blame me if she ends up lovesick. Ah! It's *sizzling*! Well, the stuff works, all right. Might as well go ahead with this. Put it on my back, will you? Put it everywhere, in fact—all over my body. I don't care if it kills me, as long as I die with whiter skin. Go ahead, slap it on. Put it on nice and thick. Don't spare the stuff!"

A truly tragic scene. But there is no limit to a proud and beautiful maiden's capacity for cruelty. There's something almost demonic about it. The rabbit calmly stands there and slathers the famous red hot pepper paste on the tanuki's burns, transporting him instantly to a world of excruciating pain.

"Nnngh! N-no big deal. I can really feel it working, though. Whoa, that's too much! Water. Give me water. Where am I? Is this . . . Hell? Forgive me. What did I ever do to end up here? They were going to make me into tanuki stew, I tell you! It's not my fault. For thirty-odd years, just because I'm dark-complected, the women have always ignored me, and just because I have a healthy appetite . . . Oh, the humiliation I've suffered! I'm so alone. Look at me. I'm a good person. My features aren't bad, I'd say."

The pain is such that this pathetic, delirious rant ends with him losing consciousness completely.

But the tanuki's misfortunes don't end there. Even I, the author, find myself sighing as I continue the tale. It's doubtful whether there's another example in Japanese history of such a cataclysmic ending to a career. Having dodged the tanuki stew scenario, he scarcely has time to rejoice before he's inexplicably scorched to within an inch of his life on Crackle-Burn Mountain. And then, after somehow managing to crawl back to his den, where he holes up writhing in agony, he's treated to a plaster of hot pepper paste on his most severe burns. Look at him lying there now, passed out from the resultant pain. Next he'll be tricked into boarding a boat of mud with a one-way ticket to the bottom of Lake Kawaguchi. No bright spots in the story whatsoever. One might venture to describe the affair as "woman trouble," but woman trouble of the meanest and most primitive sort, devoid of any panache or sophistication.

The tanuki proceeds to hole up in his burrow for three days, barely breathing, zigzagging along the border between life and death, but on the fourth day he is seized with a ferocious hunger. No sight could be more pathetic than that of him crawling from his hole with the aid of a stick and mumbling incoherently as he staggers about snatching up anything digestible. But the tanuki is big-boned and sturdily built, and before ten days have passed he's completely recovered. His appetite is as healthy as ever, his libido too rears its head, and he ill-advisedly sets out for the rabbit's hut.

"I came to visit," he says, blushing, and adds a lecherous laugh: "Woo, hoo, hoo!"

"My!"

The rabbit greets him with a look of blatant loathing. A look that says, *What, you again?* Or, rather, worse than that. *What the hell are you doing here? You've got some nerve.* No, even worse. *Damn it all! It's the one-man plague!* No, that still doesn't seem to express it. The extreme antipathy so plainly written on the rabbit's face reads something more along the lines of: *You filthy, stinking pig! Die!*

It often happens, however, that the uninvited guest is oblivious to his host's eagerness to be rid of him. This is a true mystery of human psychology. You and I too, dear reader, must take care. When we reluctantly set out for someone's house, thinking all the while that we don't want to go, that we're sure to end up bored to distraction, it's often the case that the people we're going to visit are genuinely delighted to have us. But suppose we're thinking: *Ah, that house is my home away from home. In fact, it's more like home than my* own *place. It's my only shelter from the storm!* What then? We set out for the visit in high spirits, but in this case, my friends, we're very likely to be considered a nuisance, an excrescence, and a hound from hell and to find our hosts repeatedly checking their watches. Thinking of someone else's house as our shelter from the storm is, perhaps, evidence of a certain imbecility, but the fact remains that we often labor under astonishing misconceptions when calling on others. Unless we have a particular mission in mind, it's probably best to refrain from visiting even our most intimate friends at home.

Anyone who doubts this advice of the author's need only look at our poor tanuki. Right now he's committing this very gaffe, in spades. The rabbit says, "My!" and makes a sour face, but the tanuki is utterly oblivious to her displeasure. To him, that "My!" is an innocent cry of joyful surprise at his unexpected visit. He experiences a thrill at the sound of it and interprets the rabbit's furrowed brow as evidence of empathy and concern for his misfortune on Crackle-Burn Mountain.

"Thanks," he says, though no kind words have been offered. "No need to worry. I'm fine now. The gods are on my side, y'know. I was born with good luck. That old Crackle-Burn Mountain means no more to me than a river monkey's fart, which, by the way, they say river monkey meat is delicious—one of these days I'm gonna get me a taste of that. Well, I digress, but that was some shock the other day, wasn't it? I mean, what a conflagration! Were you all right? You look fine. Thank goodness you escaped the fire unharmed."

"I *wasn't* unharmed," the rabbit says with a pointed display of petulance. "You're a fine person—running away and leaving me there trapped in that fire! I inhaled so much smoke I almost died, and I don't mind saying I thought some awfully hard thoughts about you. It's in times of great peril that a person's true character shows itself. Now I know exactly where your heart is."

"I'm so sorry! Forgive me! The truth is, I got badly burned myself. Maybe I don't have any gods on my side after all—I mean, I went through a living hell! It's not

that I forgot you were there, but it all happened so fast—
my back was on fire, and I didn't have time to look for
you because, I mean, my back was on fire! Please try to
understand. I'm not an unfeeling person. Burns are no
joke, I'll tell you. And then that Wizard's Gold or Winter's Cold or whatever it was—terrible stuff. That is one
nasty medicine. And it doesn't have any effect at all on a
dark complexion."

"Dark complexion?"

"No. What? Dark, syrupy medicine, really potent
stuff. I got it from this strange little fellow who looked a
lot like you. He said it was free, so I thought, you know,
you never know till you try something. So I had him plaster the stuff on me, but, oh man, I'll tell you what, you've
got to be careful with free medicine. Take my advice. I felt
like I had a million little whirlwinds shooting out of my
head, and then I dropped like a sack of beans."

"Hmph," the rabbit snorts scornfully. "You deserve
it. That's what you get for being such a cheapskate. 'The
medicine was free, so I tried it.' How low can you sink!
Aren't you ashamed of yourself?"

"Don't be mean," the tanuki murmurs, but his feelings don't seem particularly hurt. He's basking in the
warm, euphoric sensation of being near the one he loves.
He stands at ease, surveying his surroundings with those
cloudy, dead-fish eyes, snatching the occasional bug from
the ground and inhaling it as he makes his case. "I'm a
lucky man, though, I'll tell you. No matter what happens, I always come out alive. So who knows? Maybe I
do have a god or two on my side. I'm glad you were all
right, though, and now I'm completely recovered from my

burns, and here we are relaxing together and having a nice conversation. It's like a dream come true!"

The rabbit wants only for the tanuki to leave. His mere presence makes her feel as if she's suffocating. Eager to get him away from her hut, she quickly devises her next fiendish plot.

"By the way," she says, "did you know that Lake Kawaguchi is full of tasty, tasty carp?"

"No. Is that true?" The tanuki's eyes light up. "When I was just three years old, my mother brought home a carp and gave it to me to eat, and it was dee-licious! But carp live in the water, and, well, see, it's not that I'm not good with my hands, because I am, but I can't catch 'em. They're just too fast. So even though I know how to deli-cious carp are, I haven't had a chance to eat any these thirty-odd—I mean, hahahaha—that's my brother talking again. My brother likes carp too, see, so—"

"Is that so?" the rabbit says, her thoughts elsewhere. "Well, I have no desire to eat carp myself, but if you're so fond of them, I don't mind going with you to catch some."

"Really?" The tanuki beams. "But carp, they're fast, I tell you. I nearly drowned once trying to catch one," he inadvertently confesses. "You know a good way to snag 'em?"

"You just scoop them up with a net. It's easy. These days all the big ones are swarming off the shore of Ugashima Island. Let's go. Can you row a boat?"

"Hmm." The tanuki sighs thoughtfully. "It's not that I can't row. I mean, if I wanted to, hell, nothing to it, but—"

"Great," the rabbit says, pretending to believe his tenuous boast. "That's perfect. I have a little boat of my own, but it's too small for both of us. Besides, it's just a flimsy thing made with thin wooden planks, and it leaks. Very dangerous. I don't care about me, but the last thing I want to do is put *your* life in danger, so let's work together to build a boat just for you. You'll need a sturdy one, made of mud."

"That's so kind of you! You know what? I think I'm gonna cry. Let me cry. I don't know why I'm like this, so easily moved to tears," he says and adds, with a theatrical sob in his voice, a brazen request. "But would you mind making that good, sturdy boat for me by yourself? Please? I'd really appreciate it. While you're doing that, I'll throw a lunch together. I bet I'd make a first-rate galley cook."

"No doubt." The rabbit nods quickly, pretending to see the logic of the tanuki's self-centered assessment. The tanuki smiles contentedly: life is sweet. And with that smile, his fate is sealed. What the tanuki doesn't realize is that people who affect to believe all our nonsense often harbor evil and insidious plots in their hearts. But ignorance is bliss, as they say, and right now he's very pleased with himself indeed.

Together they walk to the lakeshore. Lake Kawaguchi is a pale, glassy expanse today, unmarred by a single ripple. The rabbit begins shaping clay from the shore into boat form, and the tanuki thanks her repeatedly as he scuttles this way and that, focused exclusively on gathering the contents of his lunch. By the time an evening breeze has awakened wavelets over the entire surface of the lake, the small clay boat, gleaming like burnished steel, is ready for launching.

"Not bad, not bad!" The tanuki prances up to the boat and first places his oilcan-size lunch box carefully inside. "You're a resourceful little thing, aren't you? I mean, you made this beautiful boat in the blink of an eye! It's like a miracle!" Even as he spews this transparently self-serving flattery, inwardly his lust is being augmented by a burgeoning greed. He reflects that with a skilled and hardworking wife like this he might be able to live in ease and luxury, and he firmly resolves to stick to this woman for the rest of his life. "Oof!" he says as he boards the craft. "I bet you're good at rowing too. It's certainly not that I don't know how to row—I mean, come on. But today I'd like to admire the skill of my woman." Insufferably presumptuous. "Back in the day, they used to call me a master oarsman, a genius with an oar and so forth, but today I think I'd rather lie back and watch. Why don't you just tie the front of my boat to the back of yours? That way the boats too, like us, will be bound as one, to the end. If we die, we'll die together. Baby, say you'll never leave me." He continues to ramble on in this crude and self-deluded manner as he stretches out on the bottom of his mud boat.

Told to tie the boats together, the rabbit freezes for a moment, wondering if the fool is on to her, but a glance at his face assures her that all is well. He's already on the path to dreamland with a lecherous smirk on his face, still babbling idiotically as he drops off. "Wake me if you catch any carp. Dee-licious . . . Me, I'm thirty-seven. . . ." The rabbit laughs through her nose, ties the tanuki's boat to hers, and spears the water with her oar. The two boats glide away from shore.

The pine forest of Ugashima looks as if it's on fire in the setting sun. And here's where the author pauses to display his knowledge. Did you know that the design adorning packs of Shikishima cigarettes was based on a sketch of this very skyline, the pine forest of Ugashima Island? I have this on the word of a gentleman who should know and pass it on to the reader as reliable information. Of course, Shikishima cigarettes have disappeared now, which means that this digression isn't likely to be of any interest to younger readers whatsoever. Pretty useless knowledge I've unveiled here, now that I think about it. I guess the best I can hope for is that those readers who are thirty-odd years or older will sigh and think, *Ah, yes—those pines*, idly recalling the scenic old cigarette packets along with their memories of geisha encounters or whatever.

Well. Be that as it may, the rabbit gazes raptly at the sunset over Ugashima.

"What a beautiful view," she murmurs.

This, I need scarcely point out, is very disconcerting. One would think that not even the worst sort of villain would have the composure to appreciate scenic beauty just before committing the cruelest of crimes, but our lovely sixteen-year-old maiden is truly enthralled with that spectacular sunset. It's a thin line between innocence and evil. Men who can drool over a nauseatingly narcissistic maiden who's never known suffering and gush about the purity of youth and what have you ought to watch their steps. That "purity of youth" often turns out, as in the case of this rabbit, to be a frenzied dance—an indecipherable, sensual mishmash that casually combines murderous hatred with self-intoxication. It's the foam on a glass of beer, and it's the greatest danger there is. Valuing physical sensations above moral considerations is evidence of either mental deficiency or demonic evil. Take, for example, those American movies that were so popular all around the world awhile back. They were full of "pure" young males and females who were overly sensitive to tactile sensations and juddered nervously about like spring-wound devices. Is it going too far to say that all this "purity of youth" business can be traced back to America? Movies like *Love on Skis*, or whatever it was. And in the background someone's coolly committing some dimwitted crime. It's either idiocy or the work of Satan. Of course, maybe Satan has been an idiot all along. I'm not certain about that, but I'm fairly sure that with this digression I've managed to turn our petite, slender, lithe-limbed sixteen-year-old female rabbit, whom we earlier compared to the heart-quickening moon goddess Artemis, into something unspeakably dreary. Did someone say "idiocy"? Can't be helped.

"Hyaah!" A queer squawk erupts from below. It's the cry of our beloved and decidedly impure thirty-seven-year-old male, Tanuki-*kun*. "It's water! My boat's leaking! Yikes!"

"Quiet. It's a boat made of mud, for heaven's sake. Naturally it's going to sink. Didn't you know that?"

"What do you mean? No! What? I don't get it. Wait. It doesn't make sense. You're not going to . . . No, that would be too fiendish. You're my woman! I'm sinking—that's the reality here, and if this is your idea of a joke, you've gone too far, you know. It's domestic violence! Ah! I'm going down! Help me out here, sweetie. The lunch will be ruined! I brought worm macaroni sprinkled with weasel poop. What a waste! Glub. Argh! Now I'm swallowing water. Hey! Seriously, enough with the nasty prank. Wait! Don't cut the rope! Together till the end, man and wife, in this life and the next, the unbreakable bond of romantic— Oh no! You cut it! Help! I can't swim! I mean, I used to be able to swim a little, but when a tanuki gets to be thirty-seven all the sinews start stiffening, and— Yes, I confess. I'm thirty-seven. The truth is, I'm way too old for you. But you need to respect your elders! Remember your duty to be kind to senior citizens! Glub. Argh! You're a good girl. Be a good girl and reach that oar over to me so I can— Ow! Ouch! What are you doing? That hurts! You're hitting me on the head! Oh, so that's how it is. Now I get it. You're trying to kill me!"

It isn't until moments before his death that the tanuki sees through the rabbit's evil scheme, by which time of course it's too late. The merciless oar comes down on his head with a thwack, and then with another thwack. The surface of the lake glitters in the setting sun, and his head appears there as he comes up for air, disappears as he sinks again, then reappears as he bobs back up. "Owww! How could you? What did I ever do to hurt you? Was loving you a sin?" Those are his last words before he goes down for good.

The rabbit wipes her brow and says, "Phew. I'm perspiring."

So, is this an admonition against lust? Or is it a satiric tale with a hint of friendly advice against getting involved with sixteen-year-old maidens? Or is it, rather, a sort of textbook of courting etiquette, teaching that it's best to exercise moderation in wooing your dream girl, no matter how smitten you might be, in order to avoid earning her hatred and possibly even getting yourself murdered?

Or maybe it's not about right and wrong at all but simply a humorous story suggesting that in our daily lives the people of this world abuse one another, punish one another, praise one another, and serve one another all on the basis of feelings—their likes and dislikes.

No, no, no. There's no need to scramble for any such literary critical conclusion. We need only take heed of the tanuki's dying words. To wit: "Was loving you a sin?"

It is hardly an exaggeration to say that all the tragedies of world literature have this question as their subject. Inside every woman is a merciless bunny, and inside every man a virtuous tanuki who's forever floundering as he tries to keep his head above water. The author, in light of his own thirty-odd years of a remarkably unsuccessful career, can tell you unequivocally that this is true. Perhaps you've noticed the same thing. That's all for now.

The Sparrow Who Lost Her Tongue

I've been writing these fairy tales little by little in what spare time I've had, what with being mobilized for civilian duty and dealing with the post-bombing remains of my house and what have you, and despite a persistent fever, hoping only that they might prove a mild diversion suitable for any moments of leisure afforded those fighting courageously to help Nippon through her national crisis. My intention was to follow up "The Stolen Wen," "Urashima-san," and "Click-Clack Mountain" with "Momotarō" and "The Sparrow Who Lost Her Tongue," and then to bring my fairy tale book to a close.

The tale of Momotarō, however, has undergone a process of such simplification, the hero himself made into such an idealized symbol of the Japanese male, that it has more of the flavor of a poem or song than a story. I was, of course, going to recast the yarn, making it my own. In particular, I intended to portray the Oni of Ogre Island as utterly depraved and despicable characters, genuinely worthy of our hatred. I would have shown them to be a race capable of such unutterably monstrous atrocities that subjugating them was simply the only option left to mankind. In doing so, I would evoke in readers such sympathy

with Momotarō and his mission, that they would be biting their nails as I unrolled a stirring description of the
battle itself—a touch-and-go, breathtakingly suspenseful
affair.

(When describing their plans for unwritten works,
authors are prone to naïve exaggeration. Everyone knows
it's not that easy. But let it go. It's all just hot air anyway.
Stifle the jeers and hear me out.)

In Greek mythology, the most repellent, perverse,
and disgusting monster of all was snake-haired Medusa.
Wrinkles of deep distrust creased her brow; the brutish
embers of murderous intent glowed in her small gray eyes;
her pale cheeks twitched with menacing fury; and her
dark, thin lips twisted with loathing and scorn. And, yes,
each long strand of her hair was a separate, live, red-bel-
lied, poisonous snake. Emitting a horrible hissing sound,
these numberless snakes would rear their heads as one to
face any enemy. One glance at Medusa and an unsuspect-
ing man would suddenly begin to feel ill; before he knew
it, his heart would freeze solid and his entire body would
turn literally to cold stone. Medusa wasn't terrifying so
much as skin-crawlingly creepy. The worst part was not
what she did to the flesh but to the heart and mind. A
monster like this deserves mankind's most righteous hatred and must be exterminated with all due haste. Compared to her, our monsters in Japan are innocent and even
endearingly charming creatures. The Ōnyūdō, with his
telescoping neck, or the one-footed umbrella goblin, for
example—they rarely do any harm but tend merely to ease
the tedium of a drunkard's wee hours by performing art-
less dances in dark old temples. As for the inhabitants of
Ogre Island, they're physically large enough, according to

the picture books, and yet when a monkey scratches one on the nose, for example, the victim lets out a squawk, topples over, and surrenders.

There's nothing the least bit scary about the Oni in "Momotarō." They even seem like fairly nice chaps, all in all, which rather takes the air out of the whole subjugate-the-ogres storyline. What one needs are monsters who inspire even more revulsion than the head of Medusa. Without such antagonists, one can hardly expect readers to be biting their nails. And then there's the fact that the conquering hero, Momotarō himself, is so overwhelmingly strong that the reader at times feels almost sorry for the ogres and experiences none of the thrill of the hair's-breadth escape. Even the illustrious hero Siegfried had that vulnerable spot on his shoulder, didn't he? And they say that Benkei too had his Achilles' heel. In any case, a completely invincible hero just isn't good story material.

Further complicating the matter is that, while I presume to understand to some extent the psychology of the weak, perhaps because I'm a helpless sort myself, I'm afraid I don't really have a clear understanding of the psychology of the powerful—particularly the absolutely invincible variety, which I've never met or even known to exist. I'm a story writer with such feeble imaginative powers that unless I myself have experienced something, I can't write a line—can't write a word—about it. It would have been impossible for me to describe Momotarō as one of those invincible heroes I've never seen. My Momotarō would have been a crybaby as a child, a weak, timid, and basically useless young man who, after running up against merciless and incomparably foul ogres who destroy human hearts and souls and drive people into hells of eternal hopelessness and horror and resentment, realizes that, weakling though he may be, he cannot back down from this fight. Taking, therefore, a truly courageous stand, he sets out for the Oni's island lair with a sack of millet dumplings tied to his waist.

Such would have been my plotline, I imagine. As for Momotarō's three vassals—the dog, the monkey, and the pheasant—they were not to be the typical faithful, exemplary sidekicks but rather individuals with uniquely problematic character flaws that would have inevitably led to the occasional squabble. I imagine they might have turned out somewhat like Monkey, Pigsy, and Sandy in the Chinese epic *Journey to the West*. But when I finished "Click-Clack Mountain" and was about to begin "My Momotarō," a sudden and terrible gloom descended upon me. Isn't it best to leave at least "Momotarō" alone, to let it remain in its current simplified form? It's a national poem, a song that has been passed down through the ages, touching all Japanese. It doesn't matter if the plot is full of holes and contradictions. To tamper with the plain and straightforward nature of this big-hearted poem would be a disservice to Japan in a difficult time. Momotarō, after all, carries the banner that reads *Nippon-ichi*—Number One in Japan. An author who has never been number one in Japan—or even number two or three—can hardly be expected to produce an adequate picture of Japan's foremost young man. The moment his "Nippon-ichi" banner came to mind, I gallantly abandoned all plans for "My Momotarō."

Having reconsidered, therefore, I would like now to wrap up this my *Fairy Tale Book* with just one more story, that of the so-called tongue-cut sparrow. In "The Sparrow Who Lost Her Tongue," as in "The Stolen Wen" and "Urashima-san" and "Click-Clack Mountain," none of the characters are Nippon-ichi, which relieves some of the pressure and allows me to invent freely. When it comes to Number One in this sacred country, however—even though it may be in the context of a mere children's story—there can be no excuse for writing irresponsible nonsense. How mortifying would it be if a foreigner were to read my retelling and think that this was the best Japan had to offer? I would like, therefore, to repeat this ad nauseam, if necessary: The two old men in "The Stolen Wen" were not Nippon-ichi; nor were Urashima-san or the tanuki in "Click-Clack Mountain." Only Momotarō is Nippon-ichi, and I didn't write about him. If the true Nippon-ichi were to appear before you, your eyes would probably be blinded by the radiant light of his countenance. All right? You got that? The characters in this *Fairy Tale Book* of mine are not Nippon-ichi—or -*ni* or -*san* either. Nor are they in any way what you could call representative types. They were born of the doltish misadventures and feeble imagination of an author named Dazai, and as such they're of very little interest. To evaluate the Japanese on the basis of these characters would be like rowing home complacently after marking the spot on your boat where you dropped your sword overboard, as the old Chinese proverb has it. The Japanese people are precious to me. That goes without saying, but it's the reason I am not going to describe Momotarō or his adventures, and I believe I have made it abundantly clear that the characters I *have* described are decidedly *not* Nippon-ichi.

I have no doubt that you too, dear reader, will applaud my oddly fastidious insistence on this point. Didn't even

Toyotomi Hideyoshi, the Great Unifier, once say, "Nippon-ichi is not I"?

Now then. The protagonist of "The Sparrow Who Lost Her Tongue," far from being number one in Japan, is possibly the most worthless man in the archipelago. He's a weakling, for starters. It seems that a physically weak man is of less value to society than even a lame horse. This man is always coughing feebly. His complexion is sallow. He gets up in the morning, dusts the paper-screen door, and sweeps out the room, and that leaves him so exhausted that he spends the rest of the day at his desk, wriggling on his cushion or nodding off and jerking awake until dinnertime, and as soon as he's finished eating he rolls out his futon and hits the sack. He has been living this pathetic sort of life for the past ten or twelve years. He's not even forty yet, but for some time now he has styled himself "the Venerable" and demanded that relatives call him Ojī-san. Perhaps we might think of him as One Who Has Abandoned the World. Those who abandon the world manage to do so only because they happen to have a little money saved up, however. A penniless man, though he may have every intention of leaving the world behind, will find that the world comes chasing after him. This self-styled Ojī-san resides in a humble thatched cottage now, but a look at his past reveals that he is the third son of a wealthy squire and that he betrayed his parents' hopes by never acquiring a profession but rather living an uneventful and meaningless life, dabbling marginally in this and that and forever either falling ill or recuperating from something. The upshot of all this is that his parents and other relatives have long since given up on him, regarding him as a sickly halfwit and a pain in the neck, but provide him with a small monthly stipend that allows him to abandon the world and still keep the wolf from the door. And though his home is a mere thatched hut, one would have to say he has a pretty sweet life.

People who live pretty sweet lives don't tend to be of much use to others. That Ojī-san is congenitally frail and infirm would seem to be true enough, but he isn't so ill as to be bedridden, and surely there must be some sort of work to which he could apply himself if he cared to. But he does nothing. He seems to read a lot of books, but perhaps he immediately forgets what he's read; at any rate, he never discusses his readings with anyone. He just sits there. His value to society is close to zero, particularly in view of the fact that after more than ten years of marriage he still has no offspring or heir. In other words, he has not fulfilled even a single one of the duties expected of a man in this world.

And what of the wife who has stood by this remarkably unambitious man all these years? One can't help but be curious about her. But were you to peek through the hedge and catch a glimpse of her puttering about, you would be sorely disappointed. She is a dreary person in every respect. Dark of complexion, she is somewhat goggle-eyed and has large, very wrinkled hands. If you were to see her moving busily through the garden, with those big hands dangling before her and her back slightly bent, you might suppose that she's older than Ojī-san. But she is exactly thirty-three, which makes this an unlucky year for her, according to the traditional view. She was originally Ojī-san's housekeeper, though scarcely had she taken charge of his house before she found herself accepting responsibility for his life as well.

"Take off your underclothes and pile them here so I can wash them," she says in a commanding tone.

"Next time." Ojī-san, sitting at his desk with his chin on his hand, replies in a scarcely audible voice. He always speaks in what is barely more than a whisper. And he tends to allow the words to die in his mouth before he finishes them, with the result that everything he says comes out sounding like "ooh" or "ah." Not even his wife, after living with him for more than ten years, can make out what he's saying, much less anyone else. It may be that, being more or less One Who Has Abandoned the World, he doesn't care whether others understand him or not. However, let us review: no steady job; no attempt to write or speak about his readings; no children after ten years of marriage; no effort to enunciate clearly or even finish his words. This passive nature of his, whether or not we give it the name "laziness," beggars description.

"Give me them now. Just look at the collar of your undershirt. It's shiny with grease."

"Next time." Again, the words barely escape his mouth.

"What? What did you say? Speak so I can hear you."

"Next time," he says somewhat more intelligibly, his cheek still resting on his hand as he peers gravely at his wife's face. "Cold today."

"It's called winter. It'll be cold tomorrow and the day after too." The thirty-three-year-old Obā-san speaks as if scolding a child. "And who do you think feels the cold more—the one who sits by the fire or the one who's out at the well doing the wash?"

"Hard to say," he replies with a hint of a smile. "You're accustomed to it."

"I beg your pardon?" Obā-san scowls. "I wasn't put on this earth to do laundry!"

"No?" he says, and leaves it at that.

"Off with them," she says. "Hurry up. You have a fresh set in the closet."

"I'll catch cold."

Obā-san throws up her hands and exits the room in a huff.

Our story takes place in the Tōhoku region, outside Sendai, at the foot of Mount Atago, on the edge of a vast bamboo forest overlooking the rushing rapids of the Hirose River. Perhaps the Sendai area has boasted an abundance of sparrows since ancient times; the crest of the famous Daté clan of Sendai depicts two sparrows amid bamboo, and in the play *Sendai Hagi*, as everyone knows, a sparrow performs a role more vital than even that of the lead actor. Furthermore, when I was on a trip to Sendai last year, a friend of mine who lives there taught me an old local children's song that went something like

> *Seagull, seagull*
> *See the sparrow in her cage*
> *When is she a-comin' out?*

It seems that the song isn't limited to Sendai but rather sung by children all across Japan. However, because of the fact that this version bids us to "see the *sparrow* in her cage" rather than the more common and less specific "wee bird," along with the hint of northeastern dialect in the last line, which fits the melody so naturally and scans so effortlessly, I've come to wonder if we wouldn't be justified in going ahead and pinpointing the Sendai region as the source of this particular traditional ditty.

In the bamboo forest surrounding Ojī-san's thatched hut, in any case, live countless sparrows, and they raise a deafening racket morning and evening. In late autumn of this year, on a morning when crystalline pellets of frost crunch musically underfoot, Ojī-san finds a little sparrow upside down in his garden, flopping about with a broken leg. He picks the bird up and carries her into his room, where he sets her by the fire and brings her some food. Even after the sparrow's leg is healed, she stays on in Ojī-san's room, fluttering out to the garden from time to time, or hopping about on the veranda, pecking at the crumbs Ojī-san tosses out to her.

"You filthy thing!" Obā-san shouts when the sparrow inadvertently poops on the veranda. She chases after the bird, and Ojī-san silently takes some paper from his pocket and cleans up the droppings. As the days go by, the sparrow seems to learn whom she can count on to be kind to her and whom she can't. When the old woman is home alone she takes refuge in the garden or under the eaves, but as soon as Ojī-san returns she comes flying. She sits atop his head or hops about on his desk or drinks from the inkstone with a tiny gulping sound or hides in the brush stand, interrupting Ojī-san's studies with her constant games. But Ojī-san, for the most part, ignores her. He does not, like so many bird lovers, give his pet an affected name or speak to it. ("Oh, Rumi, you must be lonely too!") He displays, rather, absolute indifference to where the sparrow might be or what she might be up to. But from time to time he silently rises, shuffles to the pantry, scoops up a handful of grain, and scatters it on the veranda.

No sooner does Obā-san exit with the laundry today than the sparrow comes fluttering back from beneath the eaves and lands on the edge of the desk, where Ojī-san sits with his cheek on his hand. Ojī-san looks at the sparrow with no change of expression. But this is where the tragedy begins.

After a pause of some moments, Ojī-san says, "I see," and sighs heavily. He spreads out a book on his desk. He turns a page, and then another, and then he rests his cheek on his hand again and gazes off into the middle distance. "So she wasn't born to do laundry. Still dreams of romance, I guess, with a face like that." He cracks a small, wry smile.

It's then that the sparrow on his desk begins to speak in human language.

"And you?" she says.

Ojī-san isn't particularly startled.

"Me? Me, well . . . I was born to tell the truth."

"But you don't say anything at all."

"That's because the people in this world are all liars. I got sick of talking with them. All they do is lie. And the worst part is that they don't even realize they're doing it."

"That's just a lazy man's excuse. Once you human beings acquire a little learning, you tend to become awfully arrogant. Look at yourself. You don't do anything at all. Remember the old proverb? 'Don't wake the house while still a-bed'? Who are you to criticize others?"

"You've got a point." Ojī-san remains unruffled. "But it's a good thing that men like me exist. I may seem to be good for nothing, but that's not completely true. There is something that only I can do. I don't know whether or not the opportunity to show my true worth will arise during my lifetime, but if it does I assure you I will expend every effort. Until such a time should come, however—well, until then it's silence, exile, and reading."

"You don't say." The sparrow cocks her head. "That's the sort of empty, self-serving boast you expect to hear from men who are tyrants at home and cowards abroad. 'The Venerable'—isn't that what you call yourself? Trying to find comfort in dreams of a past that will never come again, rather than hope for the future. You're pitiable, really. Your boasts don't even amount to real boasts. They're more like the grumblings of a disgruntled old crackpot. It's not as if you're involved in anything of any value to the world."

"When you put it that way, I can see your point." The old man is, if anything, even less ruffled now. "But the fact is that I'm engaged in something laudable at this very moment: in a word, desirelessness. Easy to say, hard to do. Just look at that Obā-san of ours. After ten-plus years at the side of a man like me you'd think she would have abandoned worldly desires, but apparently that's not the case. She seems to still have some notions of romance. Hilarious."

Obā-san sticks her head in through the doorway.

"I do *not* have— Say! Who were you talking to? I heard a girl's voice. Where did your visitor go?"

"Visitor?" Ojī-san mumbles unintelligibly, as usual.

108

"I beg your pardon. You were definitely speaking to someone just now. And speaking ill of *me*, at that. Well, well. Interesting! With me, you're always mumbling as if it's too much trouble to speak, but with your young visitor you're like a different person, babbling happily away in that youthful voice. You're the one who's dreaming of romance, apparently. You've gone all goopy with it."

"You think?" Ojī-san replies vacantly. "But there's no one here."

"Stop teasing me!" Obā-san is genuinely angry now. She plops down on the veranda. "What in the world do you take me for? Heaven knows how much I've put up with from you all these years. You treat me like a complete fool. Well, I'm not from a wealthy family and have no education, so maybe I'm simply no match for you, but now you've gone too far. I was still young when I came to your home as a servant, to take care of you, and before I knew it, it turned into this. I knew that your parents were good and proper folks, so I thought that being matched with their son wouldn't be such a—"

"Lies. All lies."

"Oh? Name one. Name one thing I just said that's a lie. This is exactly how it was. Back then, I understood you better than anyone. I felt that it had to be me, that no one but I could look after you properly. What part of that is a lie? Tell me," she demands, her face darkening.

"The whole thing's a lie. Back then you were all about base desires. Period."

"What is that supposed to mean? I have no idea what you're talking about. Quit trying to belittle me. I married you because I thought I could help you. It had nothing to do with 'base desires.' You say the most vulgar things sometimes! You have no idea how lonely I've been day and night because of marrying you. Is it too much to ask you to toss me a kind word now and then? Look at other married couples! No matter how poor they might be, at least they still enjoy themselves chatting and laughing together over dinner. I'm not a greedy woman by any means. I could endure any hardship and still be satisfied if you would only say a gentle word to me once in a while."

"Here we go again. I see what you're doing. Still trying to put it all on me with that same old tale of woe. It won't work. Everything you say is deceitful. You just spew any old thing, according to your mood. Who do you think made me such a taciturn man? 'Chatting and laughing' about what over dinner? I'll tell you what—their neighbors. Criticizing. Tearing others down. Nothing but backbiting, malicious gossip, all based on the mood of the moment. You know, I've never, ever heard you praise anyone. I'm a weak-willed man myself. When I'm around judgmental people, I too start to grow judgmental. That's what scares me. And that's why I decided to stop talking. The only thing people like you can see is other people's faults, and you're oblivious to the horror in your own hearts. You people terrify me."

"I understand. You've grown tired of me. You're sick of this old woman. I get it. So, where did your visitor go? She's hiding somewhere? I know I heard the voice of a young woman. With someone like that to talk to it must be unbearable to have to discuss anything with an old woman like me. You can sit there looking enlightened and talking about desirelessness, but when it's a young woman you're talking to you start babbling like an excited little boy. Even your voice changes. You disgust me."

"Fine, if that's the way you feel."

"It is not fine. Where is your guest? It would be rude for me not to greet her. I may not be much to look at, but I'm still the lady of the house here. Let me greet her. You mustn't keep stepping all over me."

Ojī-san jerks his chin toward the sparrow on his desk and says, "That's her."

"What? Stop your joking. Sparrows can't talk."

"This one does. Says some very perceptive things too."

"You're mean enough to just keep on teasing me like that, aren't you? All right, then." She reaches out abruptly and snatches the bird from the desk. "I'll just pluck out her tongue so she can't say such witty things! You always have been a little too sweet on this bird. It's sickening to watch, and this is the perfect chance to put an end to it! You've let your young visitor escape, and now the sparrow will pay with her tongue. Serves you right." And with that she pries open the sparrow's beak and plucks her little petal-like tongue right out. The sparrow flutters frantically and flies away, disappearing high into the pale blue sky.

Ojī-san stares silently after her.

And the following morning, as we all know, he begins combing the bamboo forest.

**"Where dwells the sparrow who lost her tongue?
Where dwells the sparrow who lost her tongue?"**

Snow falls day after day. But each day Ojī-san takes his search deeper into the bamboo forest. He's like a man possessed. Thousands and tens of thousands of sparrows inhabit the forest. One would think it nearly impossible to

111

find, among such numbers, one whose tongue is missing, but Ojī-san forges ahead with an extreme sort of fervor, day after day.

"Where dwells the sparrow who lost her tongue?
Where dwells the sparrow who lost her tongue?"

He has never before in his life acted with such reckless passion. Something that has lain dormant inside him would seem now, for the first time, to have raised its head, but what that something is, no one knows, not even the author (I, Dazai). A man who has always felt like a guest in his own home, constrained and ill-at-ease, suddenly finds the state of being that suits him best and chases after it. We could call that state "love" and have done with it, but the psychology expressed by the word "love" as it is commonly and casually used in daily life may perhaps be far from the wretched melancholy in this Ojī-san's heart. He searches on relentlessly. For the first time in his life he's taking decisive action and will not be deterred.

"Where dwells the sparrow who lost her tongue?
Where dwells the sparrow who lost her tongue?"

Not that he actually vocalizes these words as he wanders about in search of her, of course. But the wind seems to whisper in his ears, and at some point, as he tramps through the deep snow of the bamboo forest, this queer little ditty—not quite a song and not quite a chant—wells up in his heart in harmony with that whispering wind.

One night there descends a snowfall unusual in its scale even for the Sendai region. The following day the weather clears, and the sun rises upon a silver world of almost blinding brilliance. Ojī-san gets up before dawn, pulls his straw boots on, and makes his way to a new part of the snowy forest.

**"Where dwells the sparrow who lost her tongue?
Where dwells the sparrow who lost her tongue?"**

An enormous accumulation of snow that has settled on the canopy of bamboo suddenly breaks through, falling directly on top of Ojī-san. It catches him just right and he falls face down in the snow, unconscious. Crossing the borderline to a dream-like, phantasmal world, he hears a number of whispering voices.

"Poor man! Dead—after all that."

"He's not dead. He's just been knocked for a loop."

"He'll freeze to death for sure, though, lying out here in the snow."

"True. We'll have to help him somehow. What a mess. If that child had just gone to meet him right from the start, this never would have happened. What's wrong with her, anyway?"

"O-Teru-san?"

"Yes. I understand that she hurt her mouth, but she hasn't shown herself since."

"She's in bed. Her tongue was plucked out. She can't speak, just weeps silently day and night."

"They plucked out her *tongue*? That's depraved."

"I know. And it was this one's wife who did it. She's not a bad old girl normally, but she must've been in a nasty

113

mood that day. Suddenly grabbed O-Teru-san and ripped her tongue right out."

"Were you there?"

"Yes. It was horrible. Human beings are like that, though. They'll do the most unbelievably cruel things when you least expect it."

"I'll bet it was jealousy. I know that house pretty well myself, and this old man is awfully hard on his wife—treats her with absolute contempt. Nobody likes to see a man fuss over his woman, but this fellow's just too damn hard on his. And O-Teru, taking advantage of that antagonism, got much too friendly with the man. Hey, no one's innocent here. Let it go."

"Oh? Maybe *you're* the one who's jealous! You had a crush on O-Teru-san yourself, didn't you? You can't hide it from me. Didn't I hear you sighing one day about how O-Teru-san had the most beautiful voice in the whole bamboo forest?"

"I'm not the vulgar sort of man who gets jealous of anybody. But she did have a good voice—better than yours, at least—and she's good-looking to boot."

"You're mean."

"Now, now, you two, don't be fighting. Nobody needs that. What are we going to do about this man? If we leave the poor fellow here, he'll die. Think how badly he wanted to see O-Teru-san! Tramping through the snowy forest looking for her day after day, and then, to have it end like this—you have to feel sorry for him. He has a sincere heart, at least. I can tell that much."

"What? A damn fool, is what he is. A man his age chasing a sparrow around? Hopeless."

"Don't say such things. Let's bring him to her. O-Teru-san seems to want to see him too. She can't speak, of course, without her tongue, but when we told her he was looking for her she just lay there shedding tears. I feel sorry for both of them. What do you say we join forces and try to help them out?"

"Not me. I'm not one who has any sympathy for affairs of the heart."

"It's not an affair of the heart. You just don't understand. We want to help them, don't we, everyone? This sort of thing isn't about logic or reasoning."

"Precisely, precisely. Allow me to take charge of the operation. There's nothing to it. We'll just ask the gods. Whenever you're desperate to help someone else, against all reason, it's best to ask the gods. My own father taught me that. He said that in such a situation the gods will grant you any wish you make. So just wait here for a bit, everyone, and I'll go ask the god of the forest shrine."

When Ojī-san suddenly opens his eyes, he finds himself in a pretty little room with bamboo pillars. He sits up and looks around just as a door slides open and a doll the size of an adult walks in.

"Oh! You're awake!"

"Ah." Ojī-san smiles good-naturedly. "But where am I?"

"The Sparrows Inn," says the pretty, doll-like girl, kneeling politely in front of Ojī-san and blinking up at him with big, round eyes.

"I see." Ojī-san nods serenely. "And you, then, are the sparrow who lost her tongue?"

"No, O-Teru-san is in bed in the inner chamber. My name is O-Suzu. I'm O-Teru-san's best friend."

"Is that so? Then the sparrow who had her tongue plucked out is named O-Teru?"

"Yes. She's a very sweet and gentle person. You must go in and see her. The poor thing. She can't speak, and all she does is weep."

"Take me to her." Ojī-san stands up. "Where's her room?"

"This way, please." With a flutter of her long kimono sleeves, O-Suzu rises and glides to the veranda. Ojī-san follows, taking care not to slip on the narrow walkway of slick green bamboo.

"Here we are. Please go in."

The inner chamber is well lit. The ground outside is covered with bamboo grass through which babbles a shallow, swift-moving stream.

O-Teru is lying in her futon beneath a small red silk quilt. She is an even more elegant and beautiful doll than O-Suzu, though her cheeks are somewhat pale. She gazes at Ojī-san with big round eyes from which tears promptly begin to flow.

Ojī-san says nothing but sits on the floor beside her pillow and gazes out at the babbling stream. O-Suzu quietly retreats, leaving the two of them alone.

They don't need to speak. Ojī-san sighs softly. But it's not a melancholy sigh. He is experiencing peace of mind for the first time in his life, and this sigh is an expression of quiet happiness.

O-Suzu reappears to set out a tray of saké and snacks. "Enjoy," she says, and withdraws once more.

Ojī-san pours himself a cup of saké and looks out at the garden stream again. Ojī-san is no drinker. One cup is enough to make him tipsy. He picks up the chopsticks and plucks a single bamboo shoot from the tray. It's wonderfully delicious. But Ojī-san isn't a big eater. He sets the chopsticks back down.

The door slides open again, and O-Suzu brings in more saké and a different dish. Kneeling before Ojī-san, she holds out the ceramic bottle and says, "Another cup?"

"No, thanks, I've had more than enough. Awfully good saké, though." He isn't just being polite. The words spill spontaneously from his lips.

"I'm glad you like it. We call it Dew of the Bamboo Grass."

"It's *too* good."

"I'm sorry?"

"It's *too* good."

O-Teru smiles as she lies there listening to the conversation.

"Oh, look! She's smiling! She probably wants to say something, but . . ."

O-Teru shakes her head, and Ojī-san turns to address her directly for the first time.

"No need to say anything. Isn't that so?"

O-Teru beams. She blinks her big eyes and nods repeatedly.

"Well, I really must be going now," says Ojī-san. "I'll be back."

O-Suzu seems appalled by their guest's overly casual attitude.

"My! You're leaving already? You nearly freeze to death in the forest searching for O-Teru-san, and now that you've finally found her you leave without so much as a gentle word?"

"I'm not one for gentle words." Ojī-san smiles wryly and climbs to his feet.

"O-Teru-san, he says he's leaving. Is that all right with you?"

O-Teru smiles and nods.

"What a pair!" O-Suzu says, and laughs. "Well, please come again soon!"

"I will," Ojī-san says solemnly. He begins to walk out but stops. "Where are we, anyway?"

"In the bamboo forest."

"Oh? I don't remember seeing a house like this in the forest."

"It's here," O-Suzu says and exchanges a smile with O-Teru. "But it's not visible to the average person. We'll bring you here any time you like. You need only lie face down in the snow at that same entrance to the forest."

"That's good to know," Ojī-san says, and he means it. He steps out on the green-bamboo veranda. O-Suzu leads him back to the pretty little room, and there, lined up in a row, are wicker baskets of various sizes.

"We're ashamed not to have been able to entertain you after you've gone to so much trouble to visit," O-Suzu says, resuming a more formal tone. "At least allow us to give you a souvenir as a memento of your visit. Please choose whichever of these baskets you'd like."

"No, thanks. I don't need anything like that," Ojī-san mutters irritably, without so much as glancing at the baskets. "Where's my footwear?"

"Please. I must ask you to take one!" O-Suzu says with a sob in her voice. "If not, O-Teru-san will be angry with me!"

"No she won't. That child's not one to get angry. I know. But where's my footwear? I'm sure I was wearing a pair of dirty old straw boots."

"Those things? We threw them away. You'll have to go home barefoot."

"That's not very nice."

"Then take one of these gift baskets with you. Please, I implore you." O-Suzu presses her little hands together.

Ojī-san forces a grim smile and looks over at the baskets.

"They're all so big. Too big. I hate carrying things when I walk. Don't you have anything that would fit in my pocket?"

"Why must you be so difficult?"

"I'll just leave as I am, then. I'm not going to carry anything." Ojī-san prepares to hop down from the veranda in his bare feet.

"Wait. Please. I'll go ask O-Teru-san."

O-Suzu flies with flapping kimono sleeves back to the inner chamber. Moments later she returns with an ear of rice between her teeth.

"Here you are. This is O-Teru-san's hairpin. Don't forget about her. And please come back soon."

Ojī-san suddenly comes to his senses. He's lying face down in the snow at the entrance to the bamboo forest. Was it just a dream? But in his right fist is the ear of rice. A ripe ear of rice in midwinter is a rare thing. It emits a rose-like fragrance too—a very nice fragrance. Ojī-san carries the rice ear home and plops it in his brush holder.

"My! What's this?" Gimlet-eyed Obā-san looks up from her sewing.

"Ear of rice," Ojī-san says in the usual mumble.

"An ear of rice? At this time of year? Where did you find it?"

"I didn't find it," he says in a low undertone. He opens a book and begins to read silently.

"There's something funny going on. All you do these days is walk about in the bamboo forest and then come home with your head in the clouds, and why are you acting so smug today? Bringing that thing back with you and making such a big deal about it, sticking it in your brush stand—you're hiding something from me, aren't you? If you didn't find it, where did it come from? Why not just tell me the truth?"

"I got it at the Sparrows Inn," Ojī-san snaps.

But the pragmatic Obā-san is not about to be satisfied with an answer like that. She continues to grill her husband with question after question. Ojī-san, incapable of lying, has no choice but to tell her all about his wondrous experience.

"Good heavens. Are you serious?" Obā-san says with a disparaging laugh when her husband has finished the story.

Ojī-san isn't answering any more. He rests his cheek on his hand and pores over the book on his desk.

"Do you really expect me to believe that nonsense? It's obvious that you're lying. Recently—yes, ever since around the time your young lady friend came to visit— you're like a different person, always fidgeting and sighing like a lovesick mooncalf. It's disgraceful—a man your age—and there's no sense trying to hide it. I can tell! Where does she live? Not in the middle of the bamboo forest, I'm sure of that much. 'There's a house deep in the forest inhabited by little ladies who look like life-size dolls'—oh, sure! I wasn't born yesterday, you know. If it's true, why don't you bring back a gift basket next time? You can't, can you? After all, you made it all up. I might not doubt you if you came home from this 'marvelous inn' with one of those big baskets on your shoulders, but to take an old ear of rice and say it's the doll girl's hairpin— how do you come up with this rubbish? Confess like a man. I'm not a narrow-minded person. What do I care about a mistress or two?"

"I hate carrying things."

"Oh, I see. Well, shall I go in your place, then? How would that be? All I have to do is lie face down at the entrance to the forest, correct? I'll go right now. Or are you afraid it won't work?"

"You should go."

"What nerve you have. Telling me I should go, when it's all a big, transparent lie! All right, then, I'm really going to do it. You're sure it's all right with you?"

"Well, you do seem to want that basket . . ."

"Yes, yes, that's right—all I care about is the gift. I'm such a greedy person, after all. Ha! I know it's ridiculous, but here I go! I can't bear the sight of you sitting there looking so smug. I'll wipe that holier-than-thou expression from your face. Just wait and see. Lie face down in the snow and you get to go to the Sparrows Inn—ah, ha, ha, ha! It's ridiculous, but, oh well—I'll just follow your exact instructions. Don't try to tell me later that you were only kidding!"

There's no backing down now. Obā-san puts away her sewing and wades off into the deep snow of the bamboo forest.

As to what happens next, not even the author knows exactly. At dusk, Obā-san's cold body is found face down in the snow with an enormous wicker basket strapped to her back. Apparently the basket was too heavy to get out from under when she awoke, and she froze to death. The basket turns out to be chock-full of sparkling gold coins.

Whether or not it's because of all that gold, Ojī-san soon enters government service and is eventually promoted to Minister of State. The public refer to him as the

"Sparrow Minister" and attribute his success to his long-standing affection for those birds. But whenever Ojī-san is subjected to such flattery, he is said to reply, with only a hint of his famous wry smile, "No, no. I owe it all to my late wife. I put that poor woman through hell."

Contributors

Ralph F. McCarthy lives in Southern California. He has translated two previous collections of Dazai stories, *Self Portraits* and *Blue Bamboo*, as well as a number of novels by Murakami Ryū, including *In the Miso Soup* and *Popular Hits of the Showa Era*. His most recent translation is *Infinity Net: The Autobiography of Yayoi Kusama*.

Joel Cohn is Associate Professor of Japanese Literature and former Chair of the Department of East Asian Languages and Literatures at the University of Hawaii at Manoa. He has translated several works of Japanese literature from the eighteenth, nineteenth, and twentieth centuries. His translation of Natsume Sōseki's novel *Botchan* (1906) was co-winner of the 2006 Japan-U.S. Friendship Commission Prize for the Translation of Japanese Literature. He is also the author of *Studies in the Comic Spirit in Modern Japanese Fiction* (Harvard University Asia Center, 1998).

Printed in Great Britain
by Amazon